TWISTED TALES

2022

ADVENTURES FROM THE UK

Edited By Iain McQueen

First published in Great Britain in 2022 by:

Young Writers
Remus House
Coltsfoot Drive
Peterborough
PE2 9BF
Telephone: 01733 890066
Website: www.youngwriters.co.uk

Printed and bound in the UK by BookPrintingUK
Website: www.bookprintinguk.com
YB0512CZ

FOREWORD

Welcome, Reader!

Come into our lair, there's really nothing to fear. You may have heard bad things about the villains within these pages, but there's more to their stories than you might think...

For our latest competition, Twisted Tales, we challenged secondary school students to write a story in just 100 words that shows us another side to the traditional storybook villain. We asked them to look beyond the evil escapades and tell a story that shows a bad guy or girl in a new light. They were given optional story starters for a spark of inspiration, and could focus on their motivation, back story, or even what they get up to in their downtime!

And that's exactly what the authors in this anthology have done, giving us some unique new insights into those we usually consider the villain of the piece. The result is a thrilling and absorbing collection of stories written in a variety of styles, and it's a testament to the creativity of these young authors.

Here at Young Writers it's our aim to inspire the next generation and instill in them a love of creative writing, and what better way than to see their work in print? The imagination and skill within these pages are proof that we might just be achieving that aim! Congratulations to each of these fantastic authors.

CONTENTS

Sami Muhammed (12) — 52
Dema Al-Dulimi (12) — 53
Trikha Madhan (11) — 54
Rio Dhaliwal (11) — 55

Lewis Girls' Comprehensive School, Ystrad Mynach

Casmin Vinooshankar (13) — 56
Abby Staniland (13) — 57
Evie Hamling (13) — 58
Amy Crocker (12) — 59
Milla Bethell (12) — 60
Ellie-Louise Whitty (13) — 61
Francesca Portlock (13) — 62
Darcey Scullin (13) — 63
Taya Stevens (13) — 64
Ruby George (13) — 65

Lyndhurst House Preparatory School, Camden

Max Walford (12) — 66
David Baron (12) — 67
Mateo Song (11) — 68
Dylan Perhar (12) — 69
Oscar Lewis (11) — 70
Sebastian Holmes Hontoria (13) — 71
Rayan Choudhury (12) — 72
Freddie Peffers (12) — 73
Israel Ozoka (11) — 74
Alexander Lewis (11) — 75

Orchards Academy, Swanley

Mayowa Onakoya (14) — 76
Abigael Poulter (15) — 77
Tayla-Mae Smith (14) — 78
Ben Miller (15) — 79
Grace Warren (15) — 80
Raine Jones (14) — 81

Outwood Academy City, Sheffield

Dilbreen Ali — 82
Magdalena Cycak (14) — 83
Ryan Meakin (14) — 84
Ellie Sproston — 85
Ewan Stratford (14) — 86
Grace Widdowson (14) — 87
Robin Whitby — 88
Grace Clarke — 89
Ellis Eckhardt (14) — 90

Rutlish School, Merton

Dylan Willis (12) — 91
Isaac Gould (11) — 92
Isaac Stone (12) — 93
Ayman Taslim (12) — 94
Caleb Collins (12) — 95
Tobias Poole (11) — 96
Jude Quail (11) — 97
Matthew Ellis (11) — 98
Olly Bate (11) — 99
Ewen Moro (13) — 100
Luke Harper (12) — 101
Samuel Wenham (12) — 102
Christopher King (11) — 103
Joe Watson (12) — 104

St Andrew's RC Secondary School, Glasgow

Ayooluwamide Oluwole (14) — 105
Fatmata Diallo (12) — 106

St Piran's School, Hayle

Keira Patel (13) — 107
Karenza Isaacs — 108
Rosie Matthew (13) — 109
Toby Vogelbusch (13) — 110
Charles Owers (13) — 111

The Westwood Academy, Canley

Leon Blunden (14)	112
Ajay Fisher (12)	113
Isla Thompson (12)	114
Reagan Green (13)	115
Nathan Wilson (11)	116
Milo Kerr (13)	117
Valentino Patterson (12)	118
Rowan Mochrie (11)	119
George Smith (11)	120
Lucas Singleton (12)	121
Daniela Mackevica (12)	122
Lucas Holyfield (14)	123
Lewis Warden (11)	124
Ella-Petal Brittain (12)	125
Demi Wright (12)	126
Amelia Leather (11)	127
Rosa Stringer (11)	128

Trinity Academy Halifax, Holmfield

Aaryan Mehmood (13)	129
Favour Ilesanmi (12)	130
Rozalia Gvuzdova (12)	131
Maisie Helliwell (12)	132
Adrian Gancarczyk (13)	133
Alfie Howell (12)	134
Lois Grebstelis (13)	135
Wiktoria Rudzka (13)	136
Evelyn Rooke (13)	137
Savannah Akeroyd (14)	138
Lillie Moore (13)	139
Charlie Dolan (13)	140
Michaela Clark Campbell (14)	141
Jacob Dawson (12)	142
Olivia Stones (12)	143

Trinity School, Carlisle

Oliwier Rokosz (13)	144
Jayden Richardson (11)	145
Suri Silva (11)	146

EJ Whyte (14)	147
Lee Baty (14)	148
Lily Palmer (14)	149
Evie Phinn (12)	150
Isla Charnock (12)	151
Alex Hollins	152
Colette Walsh (14)	153
Nathan Todd (12)	154
Lucy Turnbull (13)	155
Romilly Hymers (12)	156
Jack Dalton (14)	157
Megan Gardiner (12)	158
Megan Mitchell (13)	159
Aleece Stelmach (14)	160
Sophie Duthie (13)	161
Jake Latta (14)	162
Isla Gibbons (12)	163
Sadie Haughan (11)	164
Ella Cooper (14)	165
Chloe Hall (12)	166
Lilia Kennedy (12)	167
Alex Davidson (12)	168
Alfie Jackson (12)	169
Kittie Rodda (12)	170
Dominic Pilkington (12)	171
Danielle Paton (14)	172
Logan Dowman (12)	173
Jessica Cully (14)	174
Jessica Smith (12)	175
Freddie Newton (14)	176
Jasmine Marriott (12)	177
Josie Bell (12)	178
Lily Marskell (14)	179

Tuxford Academy, Tuxford

Alexander Carter (11)	180
Charlie Sharman (11)	181
Jack Martin (13)	182
Neve Littlewood (13)	183
Leah Wall	184
Luke Shirley (13)	185
Abbie Flear (13)	186
Charles Doughty (12)	187

Erin Burke (12)	188
Anna Wheat (12)	189
Evie Howarth (12)	190
Isabela Hull (12)	191

West Kirby School & College, West Kirby

Amy Peacock	192
Riley D (15)	193
Breandán Grady (14)	194

XP School, Doncaster

Jessica Kerry (15)	195
Aaron Twell (15)	196
Kiera Leaver (14)	197
Nada Abdelbari (14)	198
Marcus Hague (15)	199
Ebony Robins (15)	200
Faith Farmery (14)	201
Yasmin Ward (15)	202
Joshua Kitching (15)	203
Francesca Wileman (14)	204
Joshua Waszak (14)	205

THE STORIES

DAY OFF

I'm taking a day off. These last few days have been so bizarre. I'll go to my favourite café in Morion to calm down and regain my thoughts. Since I won't be recognised with my new appearance, I enjoy simple hot drinks, chocolate latte is my favourite right now. I haven't even introduced myself yet. My name is Yoshikage Kira, I'm thirty-three years old and live in the northern section of Morion, where all the villains are. I enjoy living a quiet life and don't like being bothered. Although, if I were to fight, I wouldn't lose to anyone.

Struan Campbell (13)
Auchenharvie Academy, Stevenston

SELF-DESTRUCTION

They were the problem. Before they arrived, I was at peace with my creation. They destroyed my land, my home, my body. They built civilisations of their own, continuing to pollute my planet. I grew angry. The winds raged and the tides engulfed the land in darkness. The land that remained became swallowed in flames. The people were left stranded, scared. Their helpless faces almost made me feel sorry, but I already started and couldn't stop. My fury turned to guilt as the sky stayed still and dark. I was the monster. I destroyed my land and I destroyed myself.

Skye Robson (13)
Auchenharvie Academy, Stevenston

THE GRINCH WHO LOVED CHRISTMAS

I still remember when I hated Christmas. I'm so glad I have a better life now. I used to hate when the Whos would sing Christmas songs, now I'm joining in. My favourite has to be 'Jingle Bells'. I've become mayor of Whoville so I have lots of work to do for Christmas Day. I have to organise the Christmas tree and dinner where everyone gathers for a big feast. My old boy, Max, is obviously helping me with all of this, picking the decorations, the games and the food for the Christmas feast. "I can't wait for Christmas!"

Maia Lewis (13)
Auchenharvie Academy, Stevenston

GRINCH IN LOVE

The Grinch woke up on the 10th of February, realising the happiest time of the year was gone and now it was the worst, Valentine's Day. He tried to pretend it wasn't happening, but he saw cards, balloons and flowers everywhere he went. He visited Cindy-Lou to cheer himself up and met his aunt who was visiting. She was called Luri and she was crying, because no one got her a card. The Grinch saw her tears and fell madly in love. Now, they both love Valentine's Day, even more than Christmas, as they fell in love on that day.

Amy Irvine (13)
Auchenharvie Academy, Stevenston

DARTH VADER

I was never just Darth Vader. I had a life, a family until the great war. During the war, my family was killed, all of them. I was captured in action. I was the best soldier the Rebels ever had, but my skills were put to waste. When the Imperials took me, they made me join them. If I said no, they would blow the device in my neck, so I said yes. That was the day I became Darth Vader and the day my life changed forever.

Kaiden Mann (14)
Auchenharvie Academy, Stevenston

THE IDENTICAL FEET

The door opened to reveal a timid girl in rags and dirt on her face. "Hello, I'm in search of my true love." The girl's face lit up in hope, but was shattered as the prince asked, "Does anyone else live here?" Just as he said that, a young woman appeared in the doorway.

"Oh, hello, Prince Charming."

"Hello, ma'am, could you please try on this slipper?"

"Why yes." As she slipped her foot into the slipper, the prince waited anxiously. "Oh my, it fits!" she cried.

"You must be my true love!"

They hugged whilst Cinderella cried.

Anaya Hussain (14)
Bahr Academy, Newcastle Upon Tyne

6

CONCEAL DON'T FEEL

As the future queen of Arendelle, princess Elsa's life is full of responsibilities. Not to mention the question of why she always has a feeling that something is missing ever since the unexpected death of her parents. Elsa has to answer those questions, but when mysterious powers begin to reveal themselves, Elsa remembers her childhood that included a very familiar-looking girl. Elsa must take a difficult journey across her kingdom to undo a terrible curse to find the missing princess of Arendelle which could perhaps lead to a hidden truth about the girl or a truth about herself.

Jaheda Begum (15)
Bahr Academy, Newcastle Upon Tyne

SUSPECT INTERROGATION FOR THE MURDER OF HANSEL AND GRETEL

It may not look like it, but I'm actually seven. My mummy says that we look like human grannies, but I've never seen one so I wouldn't know. One day, while my mummy was out at the grave markets for fresh meat, two little humans came fumbling in. I panicked and dashed behind the counter as they wandered around. Suddenly, the one with golden braids ran to the oven and shouted, "Hansel, look! There's a cave!" I jumped out and screamed, "Don't!" but they were so frightened that they hit the grate. *Crash!* I promise it wasn't my fault!

Tahsin Choudhury (15)
Bahr Academy, Newcastle Upon Tyne

POSSESSED

Sameer had already wished for a kingdom and to be rich. What will be his last wish?

"Kid, did you summon me here just for me to wait till you make up your mind?" the genie Jafar said bored. Suddenly, he had a wicked idea. "How about you... swap bodies with me?" he suggested to Sameer. As Sameer creased his brows, he continued, "You'll be a genie and the *most* powerful." He lied. Gullible Sameer thought it was a great idea. Suddenly, as he wished and was sucked into the dark lamp, Sameer realised how grave a mistake he'd made.

Naseeha Rahman (15)
Bahr Academy, Newcastle Upon Tyne

THE OTHER SIDE OF THE DOOR

It was the time he had been waiting so long for. There it was, the perfect hour to end the control of his nemesis. Clocks ticking every second, he was finally the lost one. Moloko: the only name that's heard. Everyone and anyone who didn't obey him, bow down to him, he killed. Whoever dared to enter wouldn't be seen again and they wouldn't see the light of day again. No one dares to try taking down Moloko. He entered and slashed the throat of Steumon. His bloody head rolling on the floor. He had finally accomplished his major *revenge!*

Uzma Ahmed (13)
Bahr Academy, Newcastle Upon Tyne

HER UNTOLD STORY

In princess books, we always hear the famous quote 'and they lived happily ever after'. My story had the same cliche ending too, but no one knows about all the tears I wasted after my 'happy' marriage to Flynn. My love for him never ended, but his love did after he got what he wanted. My crown. My long golden hair is now brown and short and my aching heart increases day by day. If I've learned one thing it's that happily ever after isn't real but only exists in childhood fairy tales. Maybe mothers do know best after all.

Iqra Rahman (16)
Bahr Academy, Newcastle Upon Tyne

THE DEVIL OFFSPRING

Natas was a normal child, or so people thought. The night came and Natas' parents drifted off to peaceful sleep, or so they thought. They could never imagine the terror that was about to strike them. Silence echoed from the parents' room as their walls were painted red with blood. Their eyes were wide open yet unable to see. Natas sauntered up to his parents' corpses and began to tug at their cores, compressing them into a cup. He took a sip. Then he adopted a new farm, one that man had hated, loathed and cursed for all of humanity.

Anisha Khanam (14)
Bahr Academy, Newcastle Upon Tyne

THE FORGOTTEN QUEEN

My plan was in motion. I had taken Ariel's voice and she will never get it back unless her father is willing to make a ginormous sacrifice. The kingdom he rules used to belong to me. No one alive knows the truth, how he slaughtered my parents and people and took away the kingdom that I was meant to rule. But the truth will be out soon. If he loves his daughter, he will give me the kingdom back for his voice. Then I will destroy them for what they did. Their end is coming. Only time will tell when.

Mohema Begum (15)
Bahr Academy, Newcastle Upon Tyne

MISUNDERSTOOD

I never really belonged because of my appearance. When I was six, I fell sick, but not like other children. My illness was caused by my father who was a scientist and experimented on me, causing lots of hair to grow from my body, turning me into a beast. My parents were old, so when my mother saw me in this state, she collapsed and never woke up. Ever since then, I was blamed for my mother's passing, which is why I hid. If I could cause that much harm to my mother, I could do it to anyone.

Laila Akhtar (14)

Bahr Academy, Newcastle Upon Tyne

MONSTER

My worst nightmare is the dark. Not many people know that, as I am the one who scares them. I don't mean to but I do. I only want comfort. I turn the lights on when they turn them off. They get scared when I turn them on. I have to share a bed with them as I'm afraid to sleep alone. I get upset when they get scared but I don't know how to console them because they get more scared when they look at me. I am only a monster that's scared of the dark.

Zaynab Hussain (15)
Bahr Academy, Newcastle Upon Tyne

THAT DAY

I still think back to that day. Young and reckless. My mother wanted me to befriend Raya, she was like me, and I wanted to be friends, but my kingdom had plans to take the gemstone. I had to follow. Her face still haunts my dreams, scared and confused, because of my trickery. I wonder what would have happened if we were actual friends, or if the gemstone never cracked, sending chaos throughout our land. She may never forgive me, or even my own people. In honesty, I only hope she will save us all, forever...

Lucy Wheeler (13)
Carrickfergus Grammar School, Carrickfergus

THE EYE OF THE FIRE

Here I stand. A giant, sentient eye of mass destruction. I only have one purpose, to get the ring. I don't have a choice. I was made to do this, I don't want this. But, they're making me do this. They're making me start wars, but why? Why don't I fight back? I want them to succeed. I want them to win the war. I want them to cast the ring into the fire. I want them to destroy it. They need to do it quickly, they need to before the ring corrupts them. The ring should never've been created.

Niamh Mckinney (13)
Carrickfergus Grammar School, Carrickfergus

A PIRATE'S LIFE

When I was young, a magical boy appeared at my window. He told me tales of never growing old, but he lied. I was taken from my family to an island filled with magic and wonders, amidst other boys that placed all their faith in Pan. That faith was broken when we grew up and he tried to kill us. A few of us escaped, made it out of that evil boy's grasp and now try to protect those children that reminded us of our young, gullible and naive selves. Every day, we face that boy, narrowly avoiding death.

Gemma Moore (12)
Carrickfergus Grammar School, Carrickfergus

THE INNOCENT GOBLIN

He sat there, looking down at his green withered hands, replaying the events in his head. *It's not my fault...* he thought. *Everyone thinks I am the villain... How wrong could they be?*
In Wingston, destruction lay everywhere. People wandered past, horrified at the sight, and at the heart of them, Officer Dobson with an unusual smirk on his face. Now, this corrupt policeman was the real villain.
And so the goblin sat there, pondering whether to prove his innocence or live with the bad reputation. What should he do? I'll leave that one up to you.

Oscar Palmer (13)
Durham School, Durham

RAIN DANCE

Bound by their unbreaking gaze, they danced. Hearts leaping in time to the pounding of their bare feet across the sodden earth. Rain seeped into their skin as their faces swept upwards to meet the weeping clouds. Their shapes melting into each other's, adding a chorus of laughter to their intrinsic ballad. They dipped, ducked and gifted each other open smiles in turn. Shared memories swim in their eyes, of a simple touch. They tumbled and turned. Every time they returned face-to-face. Yet as the shower started to slow, they turned but found their partner had left with the rain.

Hannah Gordon (16)
Durham School, Durham

AN ILLEGAL LOVE

1939, a young German boy named Joseph sat with his girlfriend, Ethel. They were a beautiful couple with one major secret...

Two months ago, The War started and all Jews went into hiding. Joseph was minding his business when he heard a loud thud coming from his attic. As any normal person would, he went to investigate. As he peered into the attic he saw a dazzling and bodacious young Jewish girl.

Present day, Nazi general, Hanz, walked into Joseph's house without any warning and saw them together... He took Ethel away and left Joseph heartbroken and lost without her.

Tom Richardson (12)
Durham School, Durham

SATISFACTION

I never thought killing could be so satisfying.

For years, my enemies have feasted on my family's blood. Now they surround me. I strike one down and enjoy watching my tormentor writhe on the floor. Some might think me cruel, but how can it be wrong to fight back? I hear another approach from behind. I whip round, swing my arm and... *bang!*

Dead.

Only one remains. I press my victim to the wall and savour the moment. Those who say revenge is wrong don't know how sweet it tastes.

Besides, they're just mosquitoes. Those suckers had it coming.

James Turner (13)
Durham School, Durham

THE HUNT

As I stared into the barren surroundings, everything was ready. The plan that everyone wouldn't dare speak of, and that every living person or animal would submit to.
My plan was working, I was ready, I gave orders like the alpha male wolf to his pack. The moment was closer, I could feel fear in everyone, from broadcasters to troops.
The soldiers and I were led by the silver path of the moon. We were ready, the night as silent as death. But not for long. Footsteps deafened all around. It was time. It all started with one sound...
Bang!

Charlie Costello
Durham School, Durham

UNDER THE SEA

My mother and father took one glance at me and tossed me into the ocean, wishing death on me. Then the gods found my beaten body, brought me back to my consciousness and gifted me this fishhook. I ventured far into the universe, gaining inkings with every victory along the way. However, one challenge was not yet completed. Taking the heat of Tiffitie. I didn't mean harm in doing so. I did it for the people. Instead, it gave birth to an evil goddess, Takar. Battle was lost, and her heart lay in the ocean. It will be restored somehow.

Ajay Edwards (14)
Durham School, Durham

BURNING JEALOUSY

When we moved in with Mother's husband, we met his daughter. She had long golden hair and bright ocean eyes, we would never be able to compare. We felt no guilt treating her the way we did. The one night we had a chance, she elegantly glided onto the dance floor at that ball and won that prince. Nothing will ever stop the jealousy that burns inside me for her. Why couldn't I be the girl with long golden hair and bright ocean eyes, who can gracefully glide onto any dance floor and win the man of any girl's dreams?

Anna Richardson
Durham School, Durham

FANTASTIC MR. FOX

At long last, it was done. I shot the fox. As warm smoke rose from my gun, rising in the cold, bitter air, all was silence, all was still.

Fire was still ablaze after the rebellion. I still can't extract the image of Mrs. Fox, her children and the other animals gorging down my boy and wife. Escaping Mrs. Fox's serrated teeth, I ran as far away from the town as I could.

Later, on a storm-raging field, I saw the most beautiful, gorgeous fox on the Earth. The guilt was too much... so I took my life...

Zac Hurren (14)
Durham School, Durham

IT NEVER WAS

Last year, my friends, my brothers, tried to shoot me down. They murdered their leader's universe wide, and as far as I'm aware I was the sole survivor, why the youngest person survived, though we may never know. They say they were made to do it, manipulated and controlled, but I don't buy it. I see it as an excuse, a way out of the mess they got themselves in. Not to the public, but to themselves and to me. The public see me as the villain and them as a hero, but that's not the story. It never was.

Harry Gibson (12)
Durham School, Durham

BELONGING

I never really belonged to this place. When I first arrived at Hogwarts, I was met by all these smiles! They tried to change me, but they already knew I was a lost soul. I've planned my revenge. I will rise up with everyone who Hogwarts has backstabbed. We will rise up, we will take revenge, we will rule. I've been waiting so long. We have people on the inside, and we are ready to strike back against them. I will kill everyone single person who has tried to change my life and they'll feel my true power.

Lewis Brown (14)
Durham School, Durham

NOT MY FAULT

It wasn't my fault. Paris was so large and I just kept spreading. Locked away in the sewers, I made friends with the rats. I couldn't help that the rats got out and spread it to everyone and everything else in Paris. I never meant for this to happen. I never meant to be a plague, I wanted to be a cure. I wanted to help everyone and everything, not destroy it. I saw the world I had grown to love from the sewers ripped away, families torn apart, never to see each other again. I'm not the real villain.

Amy Gatland
Durham School, Durham

DO YOU REALLY WANT FLOWERS?

Flowers... dainty and huge, colourful and dull all lying in the most privileged or poorest places brightening up the place. A sign of forgiveness but are these wonderful parts of nature all they seem to be? In fact, they can be referred to as deadly... Some of the prettiest and nicely fragranced ones can kill you with just a simple breath. So next time you get given a bouquet of flowers don't be so happy because love can be deceiving and not all that it seems. Just like a flower you may just die away too.

Grace Jackson (12)
Durham School, Durham

THE STORY OF THANOS

Eons ago a child named Thanos was born hungry to harness the power of the universe and make everything including life. Thanos growing up was crazy and kept going on about these magic stones that had powers and tried to find them. As he left school he went looking for the crystals. On his journey, he met the Blobfish of Time to fight for all the crystals. The battle is epic but there can only be one winner and no one has ever beaten the Blobfish of Time but Thanos shall win the fight with strength and power.

Dominic Wire
Durham School, Durham

I SHALL RISE

For years I have been second to my brother, discarded to the side. For years I have been a walking second-place medal. I have endured enough. Never again will they disregard my talent, my fortune, my opinion. I vow to make them pay for the damage they so ruthlessly have created. I shall regain my pride and march my self-worth into battle until the day I am treated as an equal to my brother, king of the people. He shall suffer the loss of his kingdom as I gain it. This, my first and last vow. I shall rise.

Imogen Payne
Durham School, Durham

I'M SORRY

I didn't want to do it, it was all coming to me at once, all the lives I would both ruin and end. I couldn't turn back now. I had started this and now I had to finish it, to end the pain... I began the turn to my final destination, I felt an odd sense of comfort for a reason that I couldn't comprehend, although I didn't have much time to. I wanted to savour my guilt-filled last moments on Planet Earth, in peace perhaps. That was not going to happen, this really was the end. I'm sorry.

Harry Wightman
Durham School, Durham

PURE DARKNESS

I'm a hooded figure where underneath is pure darkness. I attack, I run away, I hide, away from the lurking dogs in their wailing cars. Yet what am I? A dark monster searching for innocent young victims or a shark waiting to catch its prey? No. I am the shadow of death. A silhouette ready to fight for what my whole life has been through. And what am I to know will await me in future life.

Through the endless times I have been through, the dogs waiting for me until I come. But I do not appear.

Isabel Sheen (13)
Durham School, Durham

REVENGE

I felt like I never belonged, I was bullied all my life. I kept going because of my idol, Batman. He made me feel amazing, all I wanted to do was be a superhero.
I grew older, nothing has changed, but there was one new problem. The bullying got so bad, I started to steal from clothes shops so people thought I had money, and my dream came true. I met Batman. I told him everything, he still thought I was a villain, beating me, making fun of my new fashion. Now I am waiting to seek revenge on him.

William Shield
Durham School, Durham

BE PREPARED...

You know my older brother left when I was younger. It's so insulting that the family just forgot about him. Suddenly, Mufasa was the future king, and suddenly I had no one to play with. My brother was never like that, he was my favourite. He always had time for me. I wanted to be just like him and still want to, but I'm not. I hate myself; if I could rule the kingdom, it would be just like he would have made it. If I had a little help, I could take power! Maybe the hyenas could help...

Freya Mole
Durham School, Durham

BATTLE ON KAMINO

There I was sitting down, but then Boba Fett came rushing in. The Jedi had found us. We had to make ourselves seem like allies. He came to me, his name was Obi-Wan Kenobi, Jedi Master. He asked me about the clones that were made out of me for an army of clones. He found out I was corrupt and evil and that I tried to assassinate the senator. We battled as Boba got on Slave One to safety. I battled the master, he was victorious. He was about to kill. Boba shot him. We escaped with my blaster.

Samuel Kanyangu
Durham School, Durham

MISUNDERSTOOD

I'm not a villain. I'm just a misunderstood hero. The world will never see me as I see it. The fear behind my eyes is covered with anger, they leave me to rot. They leave me to die. They believe what the hero tells them. I have never killed, I have never hated, much like I have never loved. I saved the hero that day, I saved him, more than anyone could. But he told the world of my selfishness, my greed, my hate. I wish the people of the villages would see me the way I see them.

Charlotte Cheesey
Durham School, Durham

THE MORTAL CURSE

"Do you seriously think anyone would believe you?" Those words droned in Flame's head.

"Nobody will believe that I would want to kill humans, I may not be the purest spirit, but they'll believe me once they say what you've done." Flame grabbed the sword from the light spirit's hand and plunged it into her heart. A thunder of footsteps came rushing in. "Orchid!" Three other spirits rushed to her side.

"He killed us both," she murmured before her body became lifeless.

"How dare you! He should be stripped of his magic." After some discussion, they made him mortal.

Jodi Gray (15)
Glenlola Collegiate School, Bangor

HANSEL AND GRETEL, THE TRUE STORY

"Here," said the old woman, her hands full of confectionery goods. Hansel and Gretal had never seen this much sugar in their lives. Within minutes, it was all gone. Feeling well-fed and sleepy, the woman led them upstairs to bed.

"Eek!" the children awoke to the woman standing in the shadows, clutching a knife. The woman ran towards them, aiming the knife at their chests. Without another thought, Gretel held her leg out, sending the woman flying towards the window.

"Argh!" Hansel and Gretel rushed to the window, only to find the woman impaled on a large candy cane, breathless.

Eden Peters (12)
Greenford High School, Southall

THE GHOSTS

Peredgine and his mother - Mallivana - moved to the old and dusty house in which his cousins lived. His mother had a breakdown and cried. The next day, she told her son what happened. The ghosts were originally murdered by Mallivana - their names were Rya and Feliz. The ghosts tormented Mallivana. Eventually, Peredgine went to confront Rya and Feliz. He apologised on his mother's behalf. Rya and Felix talked to Peredgine and forgave Mallivana. They later stopped tormenting her and left Earth with no grudge anymore. Before they left, Rya went to apologise to Mallivana, only to see Feliz stabbing her.

Shakana Ananthamohan (11)
Greenford High School, Southall

THE MISSION IMPOSSIBLE

I didn't mean for this to happen. It all started off as a normal day, well, that's what I thought until I could vaguely hear someone tiptoeing around my lab. My heart started racing. *Boom, pow.* The lights switched off. It was as dark as night. All my chairs, couches and even tables started flying around as if they were possessed. I'd never seen anything like it before. I could faintly glimpse a dark perplexing villain inching towards me. It had dark, red, bulging eyes and in the blink of an eye, it disappeared. Good riddance. It was a catastrophe.

Harvey Singh Kahlon (12)
Greenford High School, Southall

THE HOWLING PREDATOR

It was a frosty and silent night, a faint glow settled on the room. The rain pelted down on the gravel outside and a very ominous chill filled the air. The room had been abandoned for several decades, the bed inside was fraying. The floor was weathered down to mere stumps. Dark shadows lurked outside, along with the faint smell of death that hung in the darkness of the dusk. Whispers of lost voices echoed all around, creating a gloomy atmosphere. I felt a presence circling me. The footsteps got heavier and heavier. The door gently opened. It was him.

Zmar Hashem (11)
Greenford High School, Southall

STRANGLED

All was perfect. My beautiful daughter grew into a gorgeous woman, ready to fulfil my wish of becoming forever young. No more skeletal, skinny fingers or ghastly white hair, only shiny curls and smooth skin. Everything was going just the way I planned. At the start, the time I snatched her from her golden crib. That day, I knew I would succeed. But then, him, that ominous, shady thief, manipulated her with his lies and eventually turned her away from me. If she listened to me, she would be been alive today. Well, what can I say? Mother knows best.

Maja Kowlek (11)
Greenford High School, Southall

THE SINGLE CINDERELLA

Cinderella lived in a house of four. She was the youngest of her two sisters, Annabelle and Ava. Her mum and sisters always treated Cinderella like a servant. One day, they got an invitation from the price hosting a ball to find his true love. Cinderella loved the prince. Instantly, she told her mum and sisters to get ready for the ball. All of them rushed to find the finest dress. They ran into the palace. The oldest sister immediately fell in love. Shockingly, the prince liked her back. They both enjoyed their time and were happily married.

Sukhmandeep Kaur (11)
Greenford High School, Southall

THE DEADLY JUNGLE

It was a cold and silent night. A faint glow settles on the castle. The rain beat down on the gravel outside and a damp musty smell filled the air. As Faith entered, her first thought was that the castle had been abandoned for many decades. The gargoyles were weathered down to mere stumps and the garden had overgrown into a deadly jungle of dangerous insects and life-threatening plants. She had to live there because she was new to the area. She heard footsteps and she was terrified, it was too late to run. She hasn't been seen since.

Duaa Malik (12)
Greenford High School, Southall

46

THE BETRAYAL

I had to kill Damien, because Damien served me human blood for tea, Damien had killed his brother for not obeying his rules and betraying him, Damien even killed his sister for not obeying his rules and betraying him, Damien killed anyone that disobeyed him and betrayed him so I had to kill Damien before he killed me too. I was sick to my stomach to learn Damien had killed his brother and sister and served me their blood for tea. I was terrified of the demonic things Damien had done that I cannot escape the permanent memory of.

Adam Khan (11)
Greenford High School, Southall

AN UNFORTUNATE TWIST

It caught a scent. There. A flash of red. It locked eyes with its target. Then, in one quick movement, without taking its eyes off the poor girl who would now suffer an unfortunate death, it ran as fast as it could towards the girl. The girl stood, knowing it was going to be her untimely death. Yet, she stood still. Its mouth opened up, ready to devour her, but it hesitated. It sniffed... Where was the fear? Then, it cowered, for the girl was not human. Another flash of red. She walked away, a trail of blood following behind.

Jessica Bangar (12)
Greenford High School, Southall

HADES' HELL SECRETS

I never really belonged up there in the place where dreams come true and gods are worshipped. I'm not beloved like them, I'm rather thought of as the worst of them. The god of the Underworld. I've always been hated by all my family, especially my brother, Zeus. I never knew why until... At a young age, I never had a title like the other gods. I only had fire as hair, that I soon discovered could be manipulated through my hands. I could cause pain, extreme pain, so they feared me and for very good reasons.

Renaye Wells-Gardner (11)
Greenford High School, Southall

MISSING JEWEL

It didn't add up. The jewel had been a part of the royal family tradition for more than 500 years. It had remained in the same spot and no one dared to touch it. Apparently, it brought good luck to the family and, without it, a curse would be set. The room in which the jewel was stored had an insane amount of protection which made it impossible to steal. There was no evidence left at the scene. It was said that the mansion had been haunted due to the previous owners. Maybe their spirits were part of the jewel...

Stacey Matilde Carvalho Da Silva (11)
Greenford High School, Southall

THE CASTLE AND MONSTER

As I struggled to walk through the thick fog, I saw a rusty gate, wrapped in emerald poison ivy. I didn't dare to touch it but curiosity possessed me. I found a scrawny brown stick and pushed the gate open. The broken gate whined, I was so stunned by what I saw. I felt chills run down my bony spine. A castle. A half-demolished castle. I was eager to enter it but I felt like my feet were being held back. I turned around. A sublime figure, standing firmly, grabbing my legs, as if I destroyed its home.

Marium Asghar (12)
Greenford High School, Southall

THE MAN IN THE GRAVEYARD

I had to make up for what I had done.

One day, me and Tyson met a man who was going toward a graveyard. He looked a bit weird so we followed him. The gates banged shut as if it found its prey. Me and Tyson instantly felt regrets coming in here. We started to scream for help but then the man approaches us. With bloodshot eyes, grimy hands and hair filled with leaves, he told us to be quiet, because someone else was there. There was a creature coming to us. We ran, leaving the man alone.

Sami Muhammed (12)
Greenford High School, Southall

THE NIGHTMARE

I trembled in fear. This is a story of how I almost died. As I walked up to my car, I heard noises. A few hours later, the car unexpectedly stopped. My tyre was flat and I still heard noises. I went to go check it out when someone pushed me. Nobody was there, just a narrow, everlasting alleyway in the darkness, full of unknown voices. I turned around and a powerful light shone into my soul as it got closer and closer. I suddenly woke up. It was just a nightmare. My hair was out of my scalp.

Dema Al-Dulimi (12)
Greenford High School, Southall

FORBIDDEN LOVE

I had to make up for what I had done. It just happened. I didn't mean to bite her, to suck all the life and blood out of her minuscule body. I had to make amends. I had to fix my mistake. I didn't know what would happen. I felt utter guilt and thought this would relieve me. Hence, I went to gather blood from a decaying pig and injected it into her body along with the elixir of life. I sobbed into her neck, my beloved Agatha, and ran. I knew our love would never be able to survive.

Trikha Madhan (11)
Greenford High School, Southall

MY REASON

I've always been misunderstood. As a child, everyone thought of me as a big bad wolf, so as I got older, I tried to make friends, but they all rejected me. That's what I became after I grew up. I became nice again but started to get bored. I tried to make friends with three pigs and started to threaten them. I killed and ate them all. I put them in stew and tore them apart, piece by piece. That's the end of my story.

Rio Dhaliwal (11)
Greenford High School, Southall

ASWANG (A PHILIPPINE MYTH)

The shape-shifting beast who preys on pregnant women and feasts on their unborn children. Glance once at these blood-orange eyes, who knows? You might be next...
Fangs as sharp as daggers, you can feel them sink in, but you can't go anywhere or do anything... Ha, look at you... helpless.
Your screams will be heard, the blood will drip at a calming pace... *Drip. Drip. Drip...* Ah, the noise makes me relaxed... Until you've waned, the blood will drip... Drained? Out of blood? Now it's time to replace *you* with my masterpiece. Do you like it? Oh, you're dead...

Casmin Vinooshankar (13)
Lewis Girls' Comprehensive School, Ystrad Mynach

ALL THEM

I still haven't forgotten about what happened that day. I don't think I'll ever forget. I try to. But I can't. The day that everything I've ever worked for was taken from me. In seconds. It wasn't me who made me this way. It was them. It all happened because of them. Didn't it?
Yes. If they hadn't taken everything from me, I wouldn't have had to do what I did. I wouldn't have had to kill thirty-four people. The king should've just let me control the kingdom. But now there's no one left to control. Because of them. Right?

Abby Staniland (13)
Lewis Girls' Comprehensive School, Ystrad Mynach

WOUNDS

Why did it happen?

I didn't do anything wrong, why are they looking at me like that?! So frantic, petrified. It hurts.

Hurts a lot.

The wounds dug deep into my chest. Not real wounds I suppose. More eternal. Like an immeasurable cavernous slit in my throat. No wonder I couldn't speak. All I could get out were words that didn't truly explain what was happening. Words that were coming from my mouth, but not my own words. Confused? Me too. I don't know how I got in this position, however, I don't think I would like to find out.

Evie Hamling (13)
Lewis Girls' Comprehensive School, Ystrad Mynach

TAKING CONTROL

The small sweet boy act was all a lie. Why, might you ask? I was a good boy who listened in school and didn't really have many friends. I might seem like that lonely, sad boy who kept to themselves. Well, there's a reason.

Most people had those people who would tease and laugh about them every day, making them feel rubbish about themselves. Well, I was one of those people. I never really belonged, but they didn't know who they were messing with. That's where my story began of what I did to survive and how I took control...

Amy Crocker (12)
Lewis Girls' Comprehensive School, Ystrad Mynach

A HOOK

When I was younger, my mother always told me fairies were gentle and friendly, that they lived tucked away in forests with all the other magical creatures, that it's pixies that you have to watch out for.

Since then, I've always been wary of pixies when I'm sailing the seas, looking for treasure, until I saw a fairy, dressed in green, behind me as I sailed north. A smirk plastered her face as she sent me off the ship, plummeting into the alligator centre, the water. That was the day I gained a hook for a hand. I needed revenge.

Milla Bethell (12)

Lewis Girls' Comprehensive School, Ystrad Mynach

SCARE OF THE QILIN

That annoying Liron, always messing up what I want to do. It doesn't help that she is related to the God of Lions. But she doesn't know. Every time I try to assassinate the Elf, she is there. I could scare her away, she is only a child. Ariah needs to go. Or... I could assassinate her family, but would that scare her enough? What about that fairy tale everyone talks about, the Qilin? That would scare her away. Perfect. Tonight, I will tell her about the Liron-eating beast, dress up as it and scare her away. A foolproof plan.

Ellie-Louise Whitty (13)
Lewis Girls' Comprehensive School, Ystrad Mynach

MISTRESS OF EVIL

Before, I was judged because of something stuck on me that I can't change or do anything about. The day I came home and discovered my family had abandoned me for my appearance because I was different from everyone else in the village.

That was when I realised that nobody wanted me around. I was useless. I didn't want to turn out the way I did or be seen as evil, but I can't change that because I am seen as a threat. The truth is I'm not the judged young girl I was before. I'm the Mistress of Evil...

Francesca Portlock (13)

Lewis Girls' Comprehensive School, Ystrad Mynach

JUST WATCH, I'M GOING TO MAKE HER MY WIFE

I never really belonged in her eyes, but I wasn't going to give up. Some call me obsessed or psycho, but in my mind it was love. The day had come. My plan was in motion, nothing could stand in my way.

Finally, I was about to get that girl. She would be mine. But she was nowhere to be seen. She was with that foolish monster. I was infuriated with her. I gathered my men and we attacked him. She cried and screamed, but I knew she wanted me.

I still haven't forgotten the day I lost my love...

Darcey Scullin (13)
Lewis Girls' Comprehensive School, Ystrad Mynach

TWISTED TALES!

I never really belonged here in this twisted world. I had an obsession with this rapper. He inspired me. I loved him. I wanted everything to be about him. My daughter's name. I even got a tattoo with his name. He said if I wrote he would write back. He never answered. It upset me so much, my rage took over.

He didn't sign an autograph for my brother either. So I took matters into my own hands and drove off a bridge with someone in the trunk. I left a cassette for him to know it was his fault.

Taya Stevens (13)

Lewis Girls' Comprehensive School, Ystrad Mynach

TWISTED TALES

I did it to survive. I had to. Do I regret it? Maybe? They were coming for me. I had to sacrifice someone. I sacrificed my best friend. I had no choice! It was me or them. They ruined it all. My friendship, my whole life! My plan was in motion. I had to get revenge. I was finally going to take matters into my own hands. I needed to do the same as they did to my friend. It was only fair? In order for my story to start, theirs needs to end after all.

Ruby George (13)
Lewis Girls' Comprehensive School, Ystrad Mynach

THE NEW HUMAN RACE

Otto yelled, "Raven to the chopper!"
Overlord thundered, "No, Otto, you're mine. I made you."
"Never!" Otto yelled. The chopper lifted off the ground, the man diving down from the falling chopper met the propeller blades of Raven's chopper. Blood sprayed, the snow stained red.
Overlord: "I'm almost there." The metal of the silo door creaked as it opened.
Otto: "No!" Just then, Raven's chopper exploded as Otto's friends' dead bodies spiralled to the earth, then darkness fell as the missile launched. An ominous feeling. Befallen, Otto thought his friends dead. The end. Near, Overlord bellowed, "A new human race!"

Max Walford (12)
Lyndhurst House Preparatory School, Camden

THE LUMINOUS VILLAIN

There was this one unusual villain named 'The Blur' (his name was 'The Blur' because no one knew his identity). Every night he would be lurking from shop to shop and steal valuable items. He was just too swift. The city was confused about why this luminous villain stole all these items. Until this anonymous figure leaked why he was committing all these mischievous crimes. In fact, 'The Blur' was an admirer of Robin Hood and he wanted to help less fortunate people with money and food. After the news was leaked, he was known as a hero.

David Baron (12)
Lyndhurst House Preparatory School, Camden

HUNTED

The wolf slowly crept towards her target. The chicken was sleeping, unaware of her presence. If she succeeded, her cubs could survive the freezing winter. If she failed, she and her cubs would die. She pounced at the chicken, but starvation made her miss. The chicken clucked loudly in the silent night. She tried to run, but it was too late. The chicken's owner sprinted over with his hunting rifle and shot at her. The bullet pierced her chest, she collapsed to the ground. She let out one last howl for her starving cubs that echoed in the silent forest.

Mateo Song (11)

Lyndhurst House Preparatory School, Camden

I'M NOT AS BAD AS THEY SAY

Nobody would've thought I was a robber. Dressed in my Tom Ford suit and leather and suede shoes, I hopped into my matte black Lamborghini. I turned onto the familiar face of Wall Street and gave my keys and car to the valet. Investing was sort of weird because instead of making your own company, you put your money into companies that you think will thrive and make money off them thriving. However, I also had another side. I was the most notorious and infamous robber in the whole of New York's history (The Big Apple Robber they called me).

Dylan Perhar (12)
Lyndhurst House Preparatory School, Camden

MY MEALS

I was crawling around my maze. My arms ready to grab the intruder, my horn ready to pierce their heart and my flaming wings ready to grill him, I was waiting for the scent of my victim to remerge. I was hungry, I was thirsty. I needed that flesh and blood. *Sniff* went my nostrils. He smelled so delicious. I had him in my sights. Arms grabbed, his screams music to my ears, the screaming human entered my mouth. After my first chew, *snap!* There was silence. I was actually sad the screaming was gone, but I needed my meal.

Oscar Lewis (11)
Lyndhurst House Preparatory School, Camden

GAME OVER

It was a dark and scary night. Nobody was near me when the bell struck 12. A misty grey figure loomed over me as if a ghost. I dashed through with a pencil in my right hand and charged towards it. Nothing happened. Two freezing arms clutched my two shoulders. I turned my head and myself, cold, misty and grey all over. The curious something told me, "You have twenty-four hours to collect as many souls as possible. If you succeed, you can have your life back. If not, you will die." With that, he vanished into the nearby wall!

Sebastian Holmes Hontoria (13)
Lyndhurst House Preparatory School, Camden

THE PREDATOR

Sitting on the sofa, in a warehouse, bodies piled in the corner, stacks of money sitting on the table, you can smell the damp air. Out of nowhere, he hears a crunch. He grabs his gun that's sitting on his lap. Shots start firing all around him, a smoke grenade is let off, then armed men start walking in. The Predator starts firing gunshots, bodies start dropping to the ground. The leader turns around and finishes the remaining men off. "Nice to see you, old friend," says the Predator.

The last gunshot was fired.

Rayan Choudhury (12)
Lyndhurst House Preparatory School, Camden

OCTO SQUID VS CATCH GANG

Octo Suid barged through the door with power, exclaiming that I was a thief and a fraud. "You little, little Pretcal. You stole our baby Golib Golabs, our future generation." I demanded for him to go back to whatever dirty dump he came from, but he exclaimed that he wasn't going back until he got what he wanted. I knew what to do. Bring him to the floor and finish him. We charged and I seized him, plunging him to the ground. I was triumphant. I felt proud of myself and my loyal team, 'Catch Gang'.

Freddie Peffers (12)
Lyndhurst House Preparatory School, Camden

MY LAST RUN

It was pouring. Twigs screamed as their lives were crushed under my feet. I was panting ferociously. My body descended to the floor. I looked at myself in disgust. I had to get away before I was found, but doing that would be a struggle. *I have to find the exit*, I thought. My eyes darted around the room. One of the doors of a nearby dorm had swung open. The sound was unbearable. Doors kept on opening and I could hear that the gang was not much further than mine. This is it.

Israel Ozoka (11)
Lyndhurst House Preparatory School, Camden

74

THE MID-AIR HEIST

I hid in the wing of the aircraft that would be filled to the brim with gold. The plane lifted off. I crept into the cockpit and shot both pilots dead with a suppressed pistol and was piloting the plane when Rocket Man hit the aircraft and started to rob the gold, and I quickly ran into the cabin and fought him. Then I grabbed him and he flew off. I lost my grip and fell to my death while watching the smirk on his face...

Alexander Lewis (11)
Lyndhurst House Preparatory School, Camden

DECEPTION

The trope of the hero always winning ends here.
I strolled in, I'd never felt this confident. There she was.
Hanging from chains, bruised, bloody. "You look rather
horrible. Tough night?" I asked.
Looking me in the eyes, she spat out blood, a tooth. "Why
not fight me like a real man?"
With the tap of a button, she went falling to the floor.
She lunged; I pulled out a knife, pushing it through her
stomach. A loud gasp, she fell.
She laughed.
Feeling pity for a woman I resented, ten years of planning...
perhaps I might've fallen in love.

Mayowa Onakoya (14)
Orchards Academy, Swanley

MY VILLAIN

The villain in this story isn't like your basic villain. No, more like someone who ruined everything for me, like a villain would.

I'm not talking about vampires or zombies; just an everyday person. You wouldn't think a friend could be a villain in your story, would you?

Well, it is in mine.

Someone who could impact your life, bringing you to the lowest. It's not a villain in a way of killing; the only thing they are killing is the smile you place on every day.

But also a villain to yourself, beating yourself up every day for nothing.

Abigael Poulter (15)
Orchards Academy, Swanley

HERO OR VILLAIN?

One day, in the foggy mountains, Damon was piling up logs to put on the fire. Damon's a 600-year-old witch who likes to terrorise people who do bad things. He does things like killing, theft, making people go insane and memory loss. Damon lives in a place where no man will set foot. It's fog-filled, surrounding an 8,000-foot drop.
About twenty minutes after he was piling up wood, a woman came running towards him covered in blood. Bear in mind that Damon has no heart or sympathy.
Did he kill her or did he save her life?

Tayla-Mae Smith (14)
Orchards Academy, Swanley

THE STORY OF KIBUTSUJI

It's 1642, in the once small town of Tokyo and Muzan, Kibutsuji had caught wind of a demon slayer in the area. This person could make his perfect world fall, a world without violence, a world without humans.

However, the people of Japan don't agree with this ideology and train people to find and kill him. But there was one problem: Muzan was the creator, the one above the 12 Kizuki, and he is the most powerful demon. But people used to misunderstand him due to his past and his old name of 'red eyes of the devil'.

Ben Miller (15)
Orchards Academy, Swanley

DEVILISH

Everyone expects a happy story when you think of fairy tales; the bad guy is the bad guy and the good guy is the good guy. But what would happen if one day they got bored of their lifestyles and thought it was time to change?
I live in a run-down cabin in the woods, trees surrounding it for miles. I'm all alone and that's what I deserve after what I did that dark, windy and gruesome night.
If God exists, why has he cursed me with this awful beast that lives inside me? I'm worse than the Devil himself.

Grace Warren (15)
Orchards Academy, Swanley

THE CABIN IN THE WOODS

I finally got my first job as an interior designer, but it wasn't what I expected.

After a couple of hours of removing the wallpaper, I realised there were names and dates carved into it. Then curiosity got the best of me, so I started searching all the names and dates only to find out they were all names of missing people.

Immediately I rang the police and within minutes they were at the door, only to reveal to me that the wallpaper I was removing wasn't in fact wallpaper... It was human flesh.

Raine Jones (14)
Orchards Academy, Swanley

THE KILLERS' LEAGUE

"Hello, Mr Lee Cabron, you've done countless crimes such as jaywalking, and the worst of them all! Holding a salmon suspiciously. Could you justify your actions?"

"It wasn't me, it was Lamar Andrewson. I'm being framed. Literally changing all evidence to prove me guilty. Also, I invoke the fifth."

"Oh. Well, it's too late, we've got you cornered with hard evidence."

"How? There were twenty murders at the same time and I committed all of them?"

"Well... not all of them, however, you're getting executed tomorrow."

"What! This isn't fair. *No! No! No!*"

Dilbreen Ali
Outwood Academy City, Sheffield

THE DARK KNIGHT... VILLAIN?

The two figures stood side by side, watching their home town burn. One being red-haired, the other blue-haired. Both wielding opposing visions, yet still working together. To avenge Khaenri'ah's destruction, they destroyed that same god's nation. The red-haired Diluc smiled to himself. Finally, after so long of hating his adoptive brother, they teamed up to destroy Mondstadt, the nation of Freedom and Wind, once and for all. The taller figure sheathed his sword and turned towards Diluc. Once, Diluc and Kaeya had been there for Mondstadt, protecting the residents. Now it was burning away.

"We did well, brother."

Magdalena Cycak (14)
Outwood Academy City, Sheffield

ELECTRO'S REIGN

We all know how Spider-Man and Electro hate each other, but what if Electro and Spider-Man become friends? Will some people like him more than Spider-Man? I am finally going to stop Spider-Man from calling my notorious nemesis, Vulture, but first I need to get my generator.
"Hey, Spider-Man, I'm on your helipad, so let's end this once and for all by fighting against each other!"
"But if we do fight, you'll put me in prison for life, so we should really face our differences and become friends."
They both go and tell the police that they are friends forever.

Ryan Meakin (14)
Outwood Academy City, Sheffield

THE HERO?

It was the battle for it all. The perilous fight for what's right. The two sides stood face-to-face, rage building up inside of them. The wind echoed down the long dark alleyway as the two opposite sides glared at one another in suspicion. Suddenly, the courageous hero walked closer, hesitantly, towards the worn-out villain. He looked him dead in the eyes and started speaking to him. He muttered, "I'm the one who did it, but you are the one who was made out to be the villain and you got the blame. Shame that there weren't survivors."

Ellie Sproston
Outwood Academy City, Sheffield

I AM THE VILLAIN

You know that famous quote: 'You either die a hero or you live long enough to see yourself become the villain'? Well, I lived.

I was once a hero. You might say, "What happened?" Well, let me explain. I got pushed out, they threw me away... Replaced me.

I was amazing, praised until *he* came along, claiming he was the one behind it and I was just a pawn in a chess game. They believed him. Pushing me out till this day he calls me out.

"I prefer a real villain to a false hero."

Guess I'm the villain then...

Ewan Stratford (14)
Outwood Academy City, Sheffield

THE WOMAN IN BLACK AND WHITE

As I sat, eating the leftover pasta, I saw a figure walking up the stairs, dressed head to toe in black and white. That was impossible. I was home alone. My parents were out. I sat up slowly, creeping to the bottom of the stairs. "Mum?" I shouted up, scared for what was about to come. Silence throughout the house, not a single word could be heard. I jumped when I heard the phone ring. It was my mum. "Please tell me that was you at the front door, honey!" My heart could power a small city right now...

Grace Widdowson (14)
Outwood Academy City, Sheffield

THE GOD KILLER

Well, hello my friends, my name is Bultar the Soul Killer and I would like to tell a story.

Once, long ago, I was harvesting villagers' souls with my trusty scythe. Then suddenly, Zeus, the God of Thunder, arrived and threw a thunderbolt at me. I was furious. We fought for hours to prove who was the winning side: good or evil. Zeus started charging up his attack and I started throwing demon skulls at him. But it didn't work. He blasted me with his power and in the smoke I sliced him dead...

Robin Whitby

Outwood Academy City, Sheffield

THE SEVENTH LOST BOY

We all know the classic tale of Peter Pan, but what if it wasn't what you thought it was? What if it was Captain Hook who was trying to save the Lost Boys?
I was on my boat, sailing the seven seas, when Peter Pan arrived with the seventh boy. He flew overhead and I threw a rope to catch him. I missed. I leapt into the water and followed him to skull rock. I saw lights, I heard screams. A blue ember flew to the air, and the boy was now in Peter Pan's control. Now an oblivious robot...

Grace Clarke
Outwood Academy City, Sheffield

I PLAYED THE VILLAIN THEY WANTED

I never really found love. All I ever wanted was friends, but they all ran away and I never knew why. Was it my hair or was it my eyes? All I had to do was look at them and they would turn to stone. I didn't mean to do it, but everyone saw me as a villain, so they didn't believe that I really was kind, caring and most of all normal. People didn't see me as I saw myself, so I played the villain they made me to be. Goodbye, sweet Medusa. Hello, evil. Mwahahahaha!

Ellis Eckhardt (14)
Outwood Academy City, Sheffield

BETRAYAL IN MIAMI

Ms Hartsford, the assistant to CIA spy, Mitch Diamond, walked down 11th Street, Miami, Florida. She was helping Diamond try and find the anonymous drug dealer that had been causing endless trouble for the South Beach authorities. The sun was lighting up the city as she entered her hotel and returned to her room. As Hartsford walked past Diamond's room, she stopped and heard voices. Diamond said, "Everything is falling into place."
Then, an unrecognisable voice replied, "Yes, the CIA won't know what's hit them." Hartsford immediately pulled out her phone and gasped, her mind racing about what to do.

Dylan Willis (12)
Rutlish School, Merton

THE KRAKEN

I'll never forget the day I was hurled from my treehouse. Petrified, I woke in a dark, slimy sewer, luminescent green sludge spurting from the walls. Before I could gather myself, the passageway thundered and a wall exploded with unimaginable force. Instantly, I was underwater, a metre-thick pink sucking tentacle wrapped around me, pulling me towards its single malevolent eye and thrashing tooth-filled orifice. It was impossible to escape as I was engulfed by the whirling cavity...

I woke up, gasping soaking wet on my lawn. That was my dream, I expected the Kraken to strike sometime again.

Isaac Gould (11)
Rutlish School, Merton

THE GLITCH

It was a normal day. Jake launched his new game, but something went wrong. A glitch had taken over his game. In a haste, Jake tried to unplug his console, but something appeared. "I wouldn't do that if I were you," one of the characters held up a gun.
"What is that going to do?"
He pulled the trigger. A bullet fired straight out of the television.
"Please don't hurt me!" Jake begged.
The character instructed Jake to install its code onto the Internet so that he could spread a deadly virus that would bring all the machines to life.

Isaac Stone (12)
Rutlish School, Merton

THE MYSTERIOUS DIARY

Two boys were set a history project about the discussed railway. They were sent to the library but instead headed for the station to muck around. Searching the premises, they came across an old signalman's diary which told the story of a strange apparition that appeared and warned him of a potential train crash. Suddenly, they heard a thundering sound outside. Pushing out onto the tracks, they saw a ghastly face.

The next day, the boys had failed to turn up at school. The history teacher slowly opened his register and the dead signalman's diary toppled onto the floor.

Ayman Taslim (12)
Rutlish School, Merton

A HUFF AND A PUFF

A huff and a puff and darkness. That was all I remember, that pesky hair. I presumed the problem, having to be blown away constantly. Becoming aware of my surroundings, I realised my struggle. Bricks crushed, rubble everywhere. I knew I'd accidentally gusted the stick and straw houses with my breath. I couldn't help it. But, the brick house, I couldn't blow that hard. Without another thought, I knew, the pigs. I didn't know why they chose to dislike me, but they just did. No reason. Searching around, they were nowhere to be seen. I was to take the blame.

Caleb Collins (12)
Rutlish School, Merton

VICTORY IN SIGHT

Finally, he was about to win. After three years of plotting, the deranged warlock had finally come up with a plan to overthrow the puny kingdom of Wimbledon. He had placed spies throughout the tiny kingdom. They had fed him secret information while he had hidden away in the Woods of Hysteria, in his underground stronghold. It was impossible for people to find him because the mist was too thick and the undergrowth too dense. Now, he had captured the leaders of the king's army, so the kingdom was almost completely unguarded. He just needed to do one more thing...

Tobias Poole (11)
Rutlish School, Merton

MEMORIES OF A PHOENIX

I shook and stretched my body out of the ashes and embers. My mind was blank. Then I looked at the blinding flame licking the trees and a word came to me. "Fire!" Suddenly, an enormous fleeing stampede passed. I was confused so I ran after them. We travelled to another part of the forest. I tried to puzzle the past from buzzing memories, but I was interrupted.

"Back again, phoenix chick!" Several animals stared at me. "You know you're not welcome here, go or die!"

I ran away. What had I done? Where could I go? Who was I?

Jude Quail (11)
Rutlish School, Merton

A TWISTED TALE OF THE UGLY DUCKLING

Once upon a time, in an abandoned zoo far away, an ancient lizard waited in a cage. She had laid seven eggs and was impatiently waiting for them to hatch. Suddenly, six of the small round eggs hatched. They were beautiful scaly green lizards. The other colossal misshaped egg however, did not hatch, so the mother lizard worriedly and frustratingly waited. Finally, it hatched and out came a blood-red and daffodil yellow, legless lizard. For months, the beautiful lizards made fun of the legless lizard, until one day, he ate them all and it turned out he was a snake!

Matthew Ellis (11)
Rutlish School, Merton

THE WITCH OF DWALA

I'm Thores, the wealthy king who rules the land of Mercia in the continent of Eldenia. One day, I was walking in the forest when I met a mysterious robed figure. She whispered, "I'm the witch of Dwala and I curse you with safety." Suddenly, grey mist encircled me and for the next two months I really believed I was cursed. Food and water vanished before my eyes and my family and friends disappeared before me. But then I realised, those closest to me were trying to kill me - the food was poisoned! It seemed the witch's spell had worked.

Olly Bate (11)
Rutlish School, Merton

THE TALE OF THE MATTER MANIAC

I never belonged. They were envious of my superior intellect. I never belonged, even before this happened to me. Even before I became the monster children feared was hiding under their beds. When I began working at the lab, dabbling increasingly into antimatter, I hoped my work could help the Earth. I knew I was condemned when I saw the utter disgust on other people's faces. However, disgust turned to fear. My life dream was betrayed by the one I had such high hopes for. The antimatter took my body and now I live, a mere slave of its wishes.

Ewen Moro (13)
Rutlish School, Merton

TWISTED TALES

Jumping from rooftop to rooftop, the banging of the guns faded behind me. When anything was stolen nowadays, the police just went mad. If they were clever enough, they would take my photo so they could identify me. I have to eat to live and steal to eat. I waited for the man to pass, then, keeping my eye on where the police went, I crept out of my hiding place and slowly made my way to the bread stall I had come from. I climbed down the wall and straight into a police van. "Got you, rat!"
I ran.

Luke Harper (12)
Rutlish School, Merton

GOOD IS NO HOPE

I still haven't forgotten the time I became a villain. I tried to do good but it didn't work. Time and time again, I tried to be helpful. It ended in disaster, terror and destruction. I couldn't help it, so I chose to embrace it, but not at first. For some time, I locked myself in a cave, living off toenails and other grimy things. One day, I grew angry and fierce. I burst out of my isolation, causing havoc and chaos. My wrath was at its fullest; this is why I'm here, destroying Earth.

Samuel Wenham (12)
Rutlish School, Merton

PREY

I'm just a pigeon, not much in the world of birds, but there are dangers. I still haven't forgotten that day. It started out as a lovely day, but that day was difficult. I was flying from my cosy nest to find food, then suddenly, a dark shadow blotted out the sun and I recognised this bird. A peregrine falcon. I flew as fast as I could, weaving in and out of trees, in hopes to lose him, but no success. I finally flew low over the road and a car ran over the falcon. It turned to roadkill.

Christopher King (11)
Rutlish School, Merton

APOLOGY

There he was, vulnerable on the floor. We were victorious. That was until the sharp pain in my chest. I glared down to see a large blade sticking out of me. I turned my head to see my loyal-no-more companion with a devilish grin on his face. He pulled out the blade and with my last breath, I saw him feeding a healing potion to the evil leader. The world started fading to black, he didn't even say sorry.

Joe Watson (12)
Rutlish School, Merton

PARADISE?

Birthed anew from the ashes of the vengeful dead, I transcend into the Ethereal Plane. My eyes brim with contempt as I examine the mortal fools scurrying like rats down below. With my newfound omnipotence, I pluck the delicate, shimmering strings of fate, playing their pitiful lives into a symphony of twisted torment. I laugh as they toil. I scoff at their efforts. I mock their futile human struggle as an all-powerful spectator. And in return... *they worship me...* under false promises of absolution and *paradise.*

Ayooluwamide Oluwole (14)
St Andrew's RC Secondary School, Glasgow

NEVER ENDING: MY VILLAIN STORY

Years and years of this place, feels like I will never escape. Every time I see people cheering and laughing, anger rushes over me as I wanted this to be me. My blood boils in anger. *Will I ever escape this hellhole?*

The more I see people, the more I want to kill. Seeing these people happy makes me want to end them. This should be me out on the streets, enjoying my life, but instead I get locked up in this *hellhole*.

Will I ever escape? Will I ever get my revenge? Will anybody ever like me?

Fatmata Diallo (12)
St Andrew's RC Secondary School, Glasgow

HELL-BENT

Whoever said ruling Hell would be fun was wrong. I'm stuck at a meeting with Asmodeus. Finally, it's over. I start to leave when I feel a chill down my spine. I shiver. There's only one thing that makes me, Hades, the God of Death, afraid. The Grim Reaper. He's been dying to acquire my soul for centuries. If he gets it, I'll cease to exist. He'll obliterate Hell, leaving it soulless. The Reaper lunges for me, but I dodge. I run and do the only thing I can think of. Looks like I'm going back to the mortal realm...

Keira Patel (13)
St Piran's School, Hayle

HELL-BENT

I wake up on a boat. I don't remember anything. I look around and see a magnificent creature with a dragon-like appearance on top of the cliff. I now know that's why I'm here. To kill it. I rummage through the boat's contents and find a sharp rod. Climbing onto the rocks, I face the beast... Cutting off its head, it grows two back! It's a Hydra. I stab its heart and it falls to the ground. Underneath its body I see a squashed fruit. I eat it. I remember everything. I am Hades and I'm going back to Hell.

Karenza Isaacs
St Piran's School, Hayle

LITTLE ROOFUS CROW

I was always talented, I could turn anything into diamonds. Although, I never thought my power would be used against me. I found a poor man dying in the street from hunger, ergo I turned his hat into diamonds and bought him food. We grew to be close, but I realised he was using me for my talent. I told him that if he could guess my shoe size, I would be his slave. He's still guessing but, alas, I won't let him go hungry, therefore I'm destined to be his slave for evermore, for I am Little Roofus Crow...

Rosie Matthew (13)
St Piran's School, Hayle

REPUTATION

I did it to survive, I never wanted to do it but in a world where you're a god, you have to live up to the title. I destroyed Midgard, I decided to blow a hole straight through it. Now, whether this counts as mischief is a good question. I was becoming too soft, giving in to the pull of kindness. I needed to do something that would bring back my reputation. Admittedly I was only trying to destroy Mexico. But this works too. So here I am, floating in the abyss where 'Earth' used to be, talking to myself...

Toby Vogelbusch (13)
St Piran's School, Hayle

IS THE REAPER GRIM?

The 'Grim' Reaper is often misrepresented as evil and a bringer of death, but the truth is that he is not. He brings the souls of the dead to the afterlife, meaning that he is the good guy in the scenario of life, death and the one-way journey between them. If he did not exist, then there would be no messiah to guide the lost souls of the dead to the mystical place that lies beyond the grave, and the very essence of life itself. The Reaper is not grim, but he is a saint, a guide to all souls.

Charles Owers (13)
St Piran's School, Hayle

THE END OF THE WORLD

Lily May was only thirteen years old. She went to Eastwood School. In the city, scientists from the Wester Science Company, started to do an experiment. They were trying to stop people from dying, it went terribly wrong, causing the zombie virus. The chemicals of the zombie virus went into someone's cup. However, nobody realised. Three days later, the man went around biting people. Other scientists managed to escape, going into a bunker. They grabbed all the supplies from their cars and stayed in the bunker for twenty-five days. Nobody knew what awaited them when they started to go outside.

Leon Blunden (14)
The Westwood Academy, Canley

DANGER IN THE RAINFOREST

Mikayla had to redeem herself. She fell forlorn after what happened. The sky was crying with chilly rain that poured through the rainforest. It was a full moon in the twilight. A squeaky howl echoed through the musky rainforest. Mikayla carefully crept through the forest, until she tripped over a wrinkly, wet log. She looked and saw six cheetah cubs. Suddenly, a sinister werewolf galloped over Mikyla and fought the mother of the cubs, that cuddled to protect each other. The werewolf fell, the mother of the cubs chewed the werewolf until only the bones remained. The cubs were unharmed.

Ajay Fisher (12)
The Westwood Academy, Canley

MONSTER

"Blossom, there's a slight issue down in the camps, you might wanna see this," Linda said with a worry in her voice. She took me down to one of the camps and opened the door to reveal several mutilated guards lying dead, along with a note. It read 'These dead guards are a warning to you, Blossom, I've broken the monsters out, and together, we've killed all of your staff. Now, we're coming for you, Cindy'. Linda and I looked at each other with dread, wondering how we'd survive a huge army of monsters by ourselves. We were doomed.

Isla Thompson (12)
The Westwood Academy, Canley

THE MAN OF MYSTERY

One stormy night, the rain was pattering on the cobbled path, like a ballerina. A figure was lurking behind the postbox. He slowly appeared, his shadow disappearing by the second. Rain trickled down his face, the axe dragged across the floor. Blood covered the tip of the axe, like poppies in a file. He was slowly emerging, the axe making the sound of a fork scratching a plate. He got closer, seeking revenge for his mother's death, killing anyone in his path. Finally, he arrived at his destination, knocking down the door, ready to kill whoever murdered his mum!

Reagan Green (13)
The Westwood Academy, Canley

THE REDEMPTION OF THE RING

His eyes opened. Souron awoke. His minions had betrayed him and left him to suffer. They had all perished. After the ring was destroyed by Frodo, everything was diminished and left in ruin. He had travelled to the forge of Mount Doom and forged three new rings of power to crush the people of the Shire.

He travelled to Dol Guldur and the necromancer reanimated two Witch Kings, each possessing one ring each. Seige was laid upon Hobbiton that day. The Hobbits put up a fight; each Fellbeast went down with their rider. Souron was hit. The Valar forgave...

Nathan Wilson (11)

The Westwood Academy, Canley

DEEP IN THE DUNES

It was a blazing hot day in the dune desert. Most would be discouraged but not Felix. He was an aspiring young adventurer who decided to brave the harsh conditions of the dune desert, which was known for its deep pits and the horrifying dune worm. It was finally the day or Felix to venture into the desert. With a deep breath, he began his adventure. All was well until a raging sandstorm ripped through the sand Felix knew his best chance of survival was to run away, but he bumped into the dune worm. He was never seen again.

Milo Kerr (13)
The Westwood Academy, Canley

SPIDER ALICE

What if John Peaker was not Spider-Man, but Alice Splacey was instead? Alice and John entered Foolscarpe when a spider fell down from the ceiling. John dodged but it landed on Alice. Alice got on the subway and her hand was stuck to a banister. She finally got home and felt different. The next day, she went to the top of the Empire State Building. Someone fell through the glass but Alice jumped down to catch them and sat on the top. The next day, she designed a suit and went off to fight crime. She became the Spider Alice.

Valentino Patterson (12)

The Westwood Academy, Canley

TWISTERELLA

Once upon a time, there were two sisters and they worked all day until they fell asleep in the early morning. The two sisters were like slaves to their younger sister, Twisterella. Twisterella treated them both like he slaves. They had to follow her everywhere and do whatever she wanted. One day, the sisters found two pairs of Jordans and the fairy godfather teleported them to a disco. They met a prince who instantly fell in love with them. They danced all night until they fell asleep. They woke up in a ghostly palace.

Rowan Mochrie (11)

The Westwood Academy, Canley

CLUMBO

Clumbo is a big, coloured, giant lizard. People sometimes would bully him and he would get mad, angry and frustrated. Most people loved him and thought he was cute. They would feed him blue juicy berries. Clumbo would sometimes take people's weapons to give them to someone nice and if you're not nice. If you're not nice, he would be your friend, protect you, give you a present, he would help you out if you ever needed help. If you helped Clumbo and were being bullied, he would come and help you forever!

George Smith (11)
The Westwood Academy, Canley

THE END

I stared up at the factory, cursing my friends for daring me to do this. The door creaked open and I crossed the doorway, with fear building up inside me. The roof was a patchwork of holes. I foolishly decided to climb up onto the gantry up above. The gantry was bronze with rust and decay. Out of the corner of my eye, I saw a figure. They stood taller than a human and held an axe in one hand. They swung at me, murderous intent in their eyes. The axe clanged against the gantry's railing, the end was near.

Lucas Singleton (12)
The Westwood Academy, Canley

THISTORELLA

I still haven't forgotten how I got saved by the prince. He was charming. The next day, I got an invite to the ball. I wore a beautiful big blue dress and sparkly shoes. I heard a limo. I went in and it was huge. when I got inside the castle, there were lots of people there. I saw my stepsisters. The prince came and picked my stepsisters. I knew he wouldn't pick me. I was angry and annoyed at my stepsister, Emily. I shouted, "Hey! What are you doing? It's me!" Then I ran away to hide.

Daniela Mackevica (12)

The Westwood Academy, Canley

THE WOLF AND JEFF

It was one dark and gloomy night on December 6th and a boy named Jeff locked eyes with this big black wolf. Jeff stood there flabbergasted. His mother told him a story when he was a kid of the exact same wolf. His mother, unfortunately, passed away from old age so he tried to approach it, thinking his mother's soul could be living in the wolf. The wolf turned out to be friendly, so Jeff decided to take it to his house. He brought the wolf up from a cub and trained it to not do wolf-like things.

Lucas Holyfield (14)
The Westwood Academy, Canley

THE DARK FOREST

It's been two days since I was driven out of my town and away from my family. "Go hide, mi amor, I will lead them away. After, I'll find you and protect you with my life. Until then, get a new life and protect yourself." We were kicked out of our town. We were what the mortals called monsters, but we were here to protect them from the man-bear-pig. He was a killing machine. We were sent by Satan to stop him. Now, it is time to find him. I need an army to kill him once and for all.

Lewis Warden (11)
The Westwood Academy, Canley

THE ISLE OF THE CURSE

I still haven't forgotten what I have done to these lovely people. They have done nothing to me. I've been mean to them, they haven't disrespected me for years. I have not respected them. I have put a curse on them. I was so disrespectful. I need to pay up for what I've done. I will remove the curse and will stop and remove the guard dogs also. I will plot my path and get the respect of the people. Eventually, I will get my daughter from the evil school that put a spell on her.

Ella-Petal Brittain (12)
The Westwood Academy, Canley

TILDA

One sunny morning, I woke up to a loud crash. My car crashed into someone else's car. I was terrified but I was hoping to make sure my car wasn't crushed and smashed. I went downstairs to grab a bowl of cereal and ate all of it. I went on a walk to find my beautiful daughter. I had never stopped searching for her. I lost her when she was one and she is about three or four now. I found her in the woods with her family. I couldn't resist it and took her back home with me.

Demi Wright (12)

The Westwood Academy, Canley

CHARLES AND THE FACTORY

One sunny morning, I woke up and went to the shop to get my favourite bag of crisps which was cheese and onion. I was hoping to get the golden crisp ticket, but I wasn't that lucky. I went home because I was very mad. Then I got a phone call, it was the crisp factory. I answered and they said they would like me to go work there. Every time we tried a new flavour, we were all sick. Later on, I went back to the shop and got my favourite bag again, would I possibly win?

Amelia Leather (11)
The Westwood Academy, Canley

TIME FOR REVENGE

I still haven't forgotten the day she ran away with the prince. Everything I worked for was gone. Just like that. To be honest, I never meant to be mean to her, it was the only thing I knew how to do. All my life, my mum was mean to me. Now, all because of her, I work in the stupid castle, being a slave. My sister got the better half, she is married and lives far away from here. I have had enough of it. I want revenge. I have got all of the supplies, it is go time!

Rosa Stringer (11)
The Westwood Academy, Canley

THE START OF MY CYBER REIGN

Never really felt I belonged. Most of the time sitting in front of my Macintosh, my main companion. Learning, studying, coding. Kids from outside laughed at me like hyenas, throwing rotten tomatoes at my window. If only they knew who I'd become. My mum never really cared much. She was an alcoholic. She always said, "You are a mistake." The invitation came for my cyber-attack reign. There was a competition to hack a multi-million pound business that was supposed to be unhackable. Cybercriminals stared at me. Scared. Shocked. Threatened. Well, I won. But, I must hand over the malware now...

Aaryan Mehmood (13)
Trinity Academy Halifax, Holmfield

EVEN DEATH WILL NEVER SEPARATE US

"Hello, brother, do you remember how I perished and my body was never found? No? Looks like I'll have to remind you." A sadistic smile spread across the vengeful, lost soul. I awoke with an anxious feeling. The same dream over and over. The misshapen silhouette of the figure I once knew as my sister, but now became a spiteful, crazed monster, hissed happily. "Come on, brother, you want to bring me home, dead or alive. You won't be able to if you don't know where to look!" The demon in disguise sang happily, and now my journey began.

Favour Ilesanmi (12)
Trinity Academy Halifax, Holmfield

MISS DEATH

I still haven't forgotten. I still remember your grin of satisfaction. Those were the last words I heard before I did get what I wanted. I kill everything in my way and nothing can stop me. I've made sure. My beauty manipulates anyone's eyes to marry me. I've married many men to them promising full satisfaction, love and happiness. Believe me, killing them slowly and carefully was very lovely. I've used every technique in the book, nothing has stopped me from my happiness. Nothing is stopping me. I doubt he could stop me, the one and only.

Rozalia Gvuzdova (12)
Trinity Academy Halifax, Holmfield

A TAIL OF WHY I BECAME CRUELLA

I wasn't always like this. At some point, I was good. My mother used to show Dalmatians, devoting her life to them. However, at her last competition, an air of unease hung in the room, lingering like a heavy fog. There was a tragic incident involving one of her precious and beloved dogs, ending with my mother in hospital, from which she never came out. From then on, I was distraughtly petrified of dogs, especially Dalmatians. One a friend, now a fear. From now on, my life would be devoted to ridding the world of these monsters in spotted disguises.

Maisie Helliwell (12)
Trinity Academy Halifax, Holmfield

THE RISE OF JOKER

What do you think of when I say Gotham City? I never really belonged to the ordinary citizens of this menacing city. I was different, unique. As a kid, circuses were the best, specifically clowns. I would always laugh at their priceless tricks and failures. I wanted to become one. I dressed in an elaborate purple and green suit, applied bone-white make-up and blood-red eyeliner. I expected people to be amused. The opposite happened. They were frightened, terrified. When I boarded the train, they made fun of me and they laughed. My downfall began.

Adrian Gancarczyk (13)
Trinity Academy Halifax, Holmfield

THE VISITOR

A day off from killing, finally. I drifted off and recalled yesterday's murders. I was in Berlin, bellowing at the murders and planning my next. Then, it struck me. Humans relied on vision, take it all away and it would be as easy as trapping carrots in a box. If I waited until night and outed the power, no human would stand a chance. That night, I was walking down the streets of Berlin, hotels, families, everything. I was doing them a favour. The entire Berlin gone in one night. My next target will be fun. Next stop, the UK.

Alfie Howell (12)
Trinity Academy Halifax, Holmfield

BETRAYAL

We still haven't forgotten the time our good-for-nothing, stuck-up stepsister stole him from us. The betrayal. Now here we are, two years later, polishing her shoes and doing her laundry. When in the world did we ever deserve this? Mark my words, we will get our revenge, we will show her. She will wish she never went against us, she will wish she never betrayed us. She can't keep winning, eventually, we will win, we shall win at some point, stepsister. We shall, we must. We will never forget the time we were betrayed.

Lois Grebstelis (13)
Trinity Academy Halifax, Holmfield

MEANWHILE IN THE UNDERWORLD

I feel quite tired. I sit around most days. Back then, I spent them with Cerberus. But, he's gone now. I have lost everything I've ever loved. Wherever I go, it's always Hades. God of death. Evil, but what they don't see is that they are wrong. After being the villain for so many years, I'm used to it. The funny thing is I'm not even the god of death. That's Thanatos. All I wanted was to live my life in the Underworld, ruling the dead. That is my job after all. Maybe, I'll take a break today.

Wiktoria Rudzka (13)
Trinity Academy Halifax, Holmfield

THE SCIENTIST'S CREATION

I never wanted to hurt someone, but I can't make many decisions of my own. I've been created to kill and destroy. Many wish that I was dead and never existed, I think the same thing about myself. The being that brought me to life said that I was a miracle and that I would change the world forever. But no, I'm this absolutely terrifying killing machine. No one likes me, so why am I even here? I should've never been created. That scientist is so foolish. I'm not the villain or monster, it's him.

Evelyn Rooke (13)
Trinity Academy Halifax, Holmfield

ALL I FEEL IS PAIN

Living my life is hard, living any life is hard but mine is different. Mine is full of pain, anger and happiness and joy. I can't remember the last time I smiled for real. It was probably on Christmas 2012. I was four, or when I got my best friend. My only friend really. Her name is Bow, she's my dog. She's the only one I can talk to, the only one who listened and doesn't make it about them. I often sit in my room and cry, but I just feel my heart shatter into a million pieces.

Savannah Akeroyd (14)
Trinity Academy Halifax, Holmfield

REVENGE

Today I am having a day off from the serial killing that I do every other day. I am meeting my old friends that I met at school when we were young. We are having dinner at a café in town. Nobody knows who I am or what I do daily. As I walk through Halifax market, just then, I spot my old school enemy. I always hated them, they always spread lies. An idea pops into my mind. I know just the right revenge that they deserve. I laugh to myself. I am going to plan it now.

Lillie Moore (13)
Trinity Academy Halifax, Holmfield

VOLDEMORT'S DAY OFF

I was having a day off from being you know who. I woke up, put on glamour and set off to Diagon Alley. First I went to Gringotts and filled a pouch full of money. After that, I went to the ice cream parlour to meet up with the Malfoys and Severus Snape. We all got some ice cream and headed to get some new robes before we went to Malfoy Manor for a Death-Eater meeting. The meeting was boring and we found nothing out. After, I went home and went to my grey fluffy bed.

Charlie Dolan (13)
Trinity Academy Halifax, Holmfield

THE FOREST

I never really belonged. I went to the forest, further than I would normally go. The trees were tall. This was like walking into a green, gloomy scenery. There was a rustle on one of the branches. There standing, was a girl. Milky white eyes with blue forest in them. White, soft skin, she had creamy deer horns. She carried a handmade bow. Deep black hair swaying, until there was a loud noise. I looked at where it was and turned back towards the girl. She was gone.

Michaela Clark Campbell (14)
Trinity Academy Halifax, Holmfield

BEHIND THE SCENES OF CAPTAIN HOOK

Raised with no father figure and a sick mother, I didn't know how to act. Especially as I was the one to take over the kingdom. Everything seemed to be going good, Pan showed up. It was as if he was destined to make my life a living hell. I did not want to be bad, but when he used my hand as bait for a crocodile, everything changed. My new goal was to defeat Pan and to do so, I had to be extremely tough, even to my own crew. I do not regret a single thing.

Jacob Dawson (12)
Trinity Academy Halifax, Holmfield

KEEP ON GOING

No matter what, I try my best. Constantly trying my very best, just to fit in. Sometimes, I think it's no use. I just can't. I'm always attempting to make new friends and look nicer, but it's no use. I mean, it's impossible. I've never really belonged in this world. You know, people always say everyone is different and unique, but, to be honest, I am just way too different.

Olivia Stones (12)
Trinity Academy Halifax, Holmfield

COLD

It's been a while, I'll never forget what I did. I'm so cold. It's time to add the special ingredient of my videos for everyone. I'm so cold. I'll start here. This song on my guitar. It's exactly what this video needs. I'm so cold. Switching from chord to chord, somewhat fluently. I'm so cold. This house was abandoned for nothing. *Knock, knock!* It's them. I have no time. Out the door, into the overgrown grass. Why did I have to do this? This is why they're after me. I won't forget their last words. I'm so cold...

Oliwier Rokosz (13)
Trinity School, Carlisle

SHARKS

We only attack if we think you are prey. We are attracted to people splashing because we think people are in danger. Humans make us seem bad. When I realised a lot of sharks were dying, I noticed people were killing innocent sharks. The last shark attack was in November 2021. Humans kill roughly 1,000 sharks per year. There are only three shark attacks per year. People don't believe we can potentially save your life if you get into great danger underwater, people get angry at sharks for swimming in their homes, but really, humans are entering shark-infested waters.

Jayden Richardson (11)
Trinity School, Carlisle

TWISTED TALES

I never belonged. As a child, my sisters were praised for their beauty. They had light hair and crystal-blue eyes. I, of course, didn't. I was nothing but a defect. My mother aged, she grew shrivelled and ugly, until she died. Although she was cruel, her death pained me. It couldn't happen to me. Death was my enemy, so I studied and searched my entire life, until I found an escape. A herb that cured again. Unfortunately, the villagers discovered my plan and banished me They took my herb for themselves. Now, I continue to search, endlessly, forever.

Suri Silva (11)
Trinity School, Carlisle

TEATIME

The lightning thunders outside as the howling wind scratches at the window. She's here. I've missed her. I only see her when someone's passing. She makes the sad times peaceful. I wonder who she could be here for. Everyone seemed fine at breakfast. Guess we are all good at hiding things. "Hello, love, who are you here for tonight?" She doesn't answer. She only sits down and passes me a chipped teacup. I know what this means, what it shows. I can finally be hers. Forever. So I smile, sip my tea and wait for sweet eternity.

E J Whyte (14)
Trinity School, Carlisle

I DID IT

I finally did it, I killed the Batman, but what now? There's nothing left to do, I've accomplished all that needs to be done. But, I regret it. Now I'm alone, wandering the cold streets, all the sirens and people shouting, I still can't hear a thing now that he's gone. I feel there's nothing more to do. I've done what every criminal could only dream of doing. He's gone. The streets run wild, the police can't stop them. I killed the Batman. I should be happy, but it's almost like I died with him.

Lee Baty (14)
Trinity School, Carlisle

SPARK

Not cool, strange, weird, just some of the things I got called when I was young. No one wanted to be my friend. I wasn't cool, I just wanted to prove that I could be cool. No one was meant to get hurt. I just wanted some friends, someone there for me. I was the disappointment of the family. "You're a disgrace, Max, no wonder no one's your friend." Well, look at me now, Dad, I'm Electro. I can get friends now I'm cool. Who's the disappointment now? I even met Spider-Man. No one was meant to get hurt.

Lily Palmer (14)
Trinity School, Carlisle

THE MINOTAUR

The way he controlled me, changed me, made me a murderer. I was tricked. I was so innocent, not a word to my name. Never again. My good friend, Minos, and I decided to set up a challenge. I was trapped in this maze, endlessly searching. Bodies, innocent bodies that I'd slaughtered to see my daughter. "Just once, please? Just one more?" he said. I reluctantly agreed. One after one, the days, I'd lost count, until I heard her. My daughter. She was so close, I cried. It wasn't her. He laughed. It was battle time.

Evie Phinn (12)
Trinity School, Carlisle

GONE

I never really belonged, but that doesn't mean I should be robbed of my childhood. I was a vulnerable five-year-old child with hopes and dreams. All I wanted was to live a happy and fortunate life. I never meant to cause fear for the humans around me, I was misunderstood. Being trapped in a glass case, day after day, with nothing to do, is extremely boring. So, when the opportunity came to be free, I took it. Freedom felt amazing. Finally, I was about to win, about to get my childhood back. Suddenly, my happiness drained away.

Isla Charnock (12)
Trinity School, Carlisle

SORRY

I have just lost my beloved wife. I was in tears and frustrated. Suddenly, a luminous portal opened in my rusty, worn wardrobe. I went through, quickly hoping for some good luck. Before I knew it, people were sprinting towards me. With no mercy, I knocked them all out. My knuckles were red and I was bleeding like Hell's door. Then I saw a figure in the distance. It was her. I grabbed her and got out of there. But my wife started crying out loud, saying, "Those were innocent people!" These were her very last words.

Alex Hollins

Trinity School, Carlisle

FLOWER

The end! Or so you thought. The prince marries the princess and peace is restored. However, I'm seen as a villain, a monster who kidnapped the princess. But, it was them who stole from me. That flower was mine, it kept me young and beautiful. But the queen fell ill and stole my flower. I grew weak without it. The only way to get my youth back was to get the child. I locked her in the tower to protect her. Imagine if someone that didn't understand her saw her magic hair. Raising her as my own, they're the villains.

Colette Walsh (14)

Trinity School, Carlisle

WHO WOULD BELIEVE A KILLER?

I still haven't forgotten my past, the people I've hurt, the things I've done. While it might not seem like it, I've changed. It was all a mistake. I got excitement like no other when I saw suffering the excitement my sister gave me. That was until she died in my arms. I could only replicate that by killing. My grief took over and it went on for years. Eventually, I came to my senses and told my friend. Soon after, I was in prison. I wanted to make things right, but who would ever believe a serial killer?

Nathan Todd (12)
Trinity School, Carlisle

MALEFICENT

That superhero act was all a lie. I was born, put into the world and then just named the villain of the story. Even before I became more powerful, I was manipulated and used for my long, luxurious wings, by a prince! The king and queen told all the townspeople I was evil and cruel, when in fact, I was innocent. I lost my mother and father and was completely and utterly alone my whole life. The so-called saviour prince... I had no one, they had it all. A castle, supporters, family there, so, who was the real villain?

Lucy Turnbull (13)
Trinity School, Carlisle

PUTIN'S STORY

Vladimir Putin's life was a struggle. His dad always told him the world could be his one day, he could rule the world without a doubt. He kept perusing this dream of this and started wars. Some lost, some won. But then, he started the worst war anybody had seen, Ukraine vs Russia. No matter how many deaths he heard about or saw, he still kept fighting with that dream. One day, he would rule the world. Still, today, the war had still happened. He wanted his dream to one day control the world, in his fake life.

Romilly Hymers (12)
Trinity School, Carlisle

DAY OFF

It was my day off and I had just woken up after taking over the world. My servants brought me breakfast but then Batman jumped into my room, looking for a fight. I stumbled out of my bed, shocked at what just happened. I quickly ran, trying to escape his deadly grasp. He flung me across the room, shouting, "You will pay for what you've done!" He carried me out of the room into the outdoors. People cheered his name. I was disgusted by what they said. Now, I had to live with the feeling of defeat...

Jack Dalton (14)
Trinity School, Carlisle

REDEMPTION

I did it to survive. It's been three long months since I robbed that bank. I did it because I couldn't afford to live in my house. I couldn't deal with my kids living on the street. I knew after that I was a bad person, but I couldn't do anything. I paid off the mortgage but I still wasn't happy. I waited one month until I decided to turn myself in. I handed the rest of the money hoping people would forgive me. I would never know if people would ever fully trust that I had really changed.

Megan Gardiner (12)
Trinity School, Carlisle

WHO IS THE VILLAIN?

I don't mean to be like this. I don't mean to kidnap children. No one understands. Having a daughter was the best thing that ever happened to me, but the love didn't compare to the pain I felt when I lost her. Every day, I wake up, longing for that warmth to fill me once more. But, deep in my heart, I know that no child can replace my own. They all run away screaming, shouting and crying to their mums, who look at me disgusted. They think I'm the villain. There is only one true villain, love.

Megan Mitchell (13)
Trinity School, Carlisle

THE THINGS YOU DO FOR LOVE

There she was, the most beautiful girl in the world, but I wanted to tear her limb from limb and suck her dry. Her blood trickled through her body like a lake. My urge to run and bite her was filling me up like oxygen. Her hair was blonde and long. Her big blue eyes glimmered in the sun. She was shaped like an hourglass. I wanted her to be mine. The smell ran under my nose, the smell of breathtaking blood. I couldn't control myself. I ran for her, she lay helplessly in the street. I'm sorry, my girl.

Aleece Stelmach (14)
Trinity School, Carlisle

DESERVED

My father had always told me myths about magical mermaids that lived in the depths of the ocean. I would always wonder if they were truly out there. Until I saw one out by the shore. I begged for them to turn me into one of them. They agreed and started chanting and singing. As I looked down, instead of having a gorgeous, scaled, mermaid tail, I had huge disgusting tentacles. Ever since that day, I have never trusted anyone. I look down, away at the bottom of the sea, seeking revenge, that I know I deserve.

Sophie Duthie (13)
Trinity School, Carlisle

REDEMPTION

I had to make up for what I had done. I pleaded with him to forgive me. He did. I needed to prove I want just the villain and show I could change. To start, I helped old ladies cross the road and got cats out of trees. Then, I was stopping bank robberies and saved the president. Even he now respected me. I was his apprentice. It happened so quickly, we were saving people and they appeared. We had to fight them off, harder than anything else. The blast was about to hit him. I leapt, then, total darkness.

Jake Latta (14)
Trinity School, Carlisle

MOTHER GOTHEL

When I was younger, my parents never cared for me. They always left me to myself and eventually I got fed up. I had to run away. After running away, I wandered into a forest and found a tower. I locked myself inside for years, in case someone found me, but, eventually, I went insane and needed some company. I wandered into the forest and walked towards the fast-flowing river. I saw a couple with a baby rolling around on the grass. I had to take my chance. I quickly grabbed the baby and ran off with her.

Isla Gibbons (12)
Trinity School, Carlisle

I DID IT TO SURVIVE

It gives me passion, a feeling of relief, the same one I got when my father was still alive. Seeing people suffer. After ten years in jail, everyone knew my name, not my past. I realised it needed changing. While visiting my father, I saw a small boy fall. I walked closer to help the boy, then screams, "Please don't hurt me!" A tear rolled down my cheek as I realised I was seen as a monster. His mother ran to him and quickly walked away. I was trying to help, but who would believe me?

Sadie Haughan (11)
Trinity School, Carlisle

I'M NOT A KILLER

I'm sick of people. People who do bad things and get away with it. People who don't care for the pain that they've caused. Specifically men. I let them in, they break my heart, leaving me cold and empty time after time. They do bad things and just get to walk away! They must learn. One day, he's pushing me, punching me, bruising me. I feel helpless, my heart racing, my thoughts freezing. I grab the kitchen knife and what else can I do? At least now he can stop hurting people.

Ella Cooper (14)
Trinity School, Carlisle

I DID IT TO SURVIVE

I did it to survive. I did it for freedom. I was bullied as a child and did horrible things. I was taken and turned into this horrible creature. I loved to watch people suffer. I loved to watch people fight for their lives. It made me happy. No one could ever make people suffer as I could. Let's just say, no one had a bigger kill chart than me. Until that one day, my own trick tricked me. I wasn't the only one there, my best friend was there. I did what I had to do, to survive.

Chloe Hall (12)
Trinity School, Carlisle

MY MOTHER

As a child, I was very close with my mother, we were best friends. I never really belonged so I just stayed home. When I was young, I would do everything with her and I would always watch her sew buttons. I got very good. Eventually, my mother sadly died when I was eleven. It was horrible. I decided that I was going to be the best mum ever for my child. I got older and had an amazing child, but sadly she died last year. So now, I take other children and sew buttons onto their eyes.

Lilia Kennedy (12)
Trinity School, Carlisle

KILL EVERYTHING

I never really belonged after I crashed into the Amazon Rainforest, but, enough about me. Let's go back to where it all started. As I opened the door to the escape pod, I heard the distant scream of my father and mother, and then off I went. As I entered the Earth's atmosphere, I saw the fault button light up as I hit the ground. I heard the sound of suppressed pistols so I hopped into the pod and put my thermal mask on. I killed everyone in sight so no one was left living.

Alex Davidson (12)
Trinity School, Carlisle

BIKINI BOTTOM

I never really felt like I belonged in Bikini Bottom. Everyone was being rude to me and SpongeBob now hated me since he got fired from the Krusty Krab. He became violent toward me but he did something I would never forget. He smashed my shell in half. I ran away. I was free. This suffering ended so I thought some sort of demon came out of my shell and into my body. It was pain. He said, "We must get revenge on SpongeBob and the whole of Bikini Bottom for what happened..."

Alfie Jackson (12)
Trinity School, Carlisle

THE LIZARD PERSON

I did it to survive. I was miserable and didn't like people, especially kids, because I had wings and people would look at me funny. Then one day a little boy came up to me and asked for a ride. I looked and grinned. I agreed. He wasn't seen again. I decided to pay the parents back. After six years of keeping a child hostage, I took him home. Something went wrong in the plan. When I took him home, his parents weren't there, so I decided just to eat him for my lunch.

Kittie Rodda (12)
Trinity School, Carlisle

NOT MY JOB

As I march down towards my leader, fear fills my body. I suffer from the guilt of what I have done in the past. I can't do this job, I have to stop. This time, my orders are to brutally torture and murder a group of Jedi. I don't know why I am in this job, but I do it to survive. I fly to the Jedi camp, sweat dripping from head to toe. I pull out my sharp axe. Through the bodies of innocents. Blood dripping from my face. I do it to survive, but I'm the bad guy.

Dominic Pilkington (12)
Trinity School, Carlisle

THE VILLAIN OF NIGHTMARE BEGINS

I never really belonged in a world with such villains. They are all scary and evil. I turned around and saw another stranger acting scared. I went over and we became a team. We heard noises so we ran as fast as a tiger. In a blink of an eye, a villain came out and made us fall to the floor. We were surrounded by them. After a few minutes, my partner got attacked and turned into a villain. I was so scared. After, they came up with a plan and attacked me. I was no human!

Danielle Paton (14)
Trinity School, Carlisle

TRAPPED

I was talking to my best friend, but then, we had an argument and he ran off. After that day, I've never seen him again. When I got back home, I saw the village on fire. I knew who it was, but how? Then I realised that he burnt it down and saved the people, to make it look like he was a hero. I went to his house and rang the doorbell. He opened the door. He let me in and locked the door behind me. I went down the stairs into a dungeon. He laughed. I was trapped.

Logan Dowman (12)
Trinity School, Carlisle

KILLER

My dorsal fin collapse is an example of the desolation I feel. They say it's my fault. Try living in a bathtub all of your life, see how long you will last. They blame me even though they enslaved me and forced me to be a circus performer when I was once a graceful giant of the ocean. Reduced to a mistreated goldfish. The name, killer whale, does not reflect me. From my black and white monochrome skin, down to my misshapen fins, my scars and injuries.

Jessica Cully (14)
Trinity School, Carlisle

MEMORY

Finally, as she sat down and noticed what she had done over the past couple of years, her mind got the better of her and took her way back to the start, her house. Before her eyes were buttons and the daughter that she left behind years ago, in the cupboard under the stairs. As she opened the hatch, her daughter screamed as loud as the wind and in pain. She shut the door in pain and it took her right back to the days when everything was normal in life.

Jessica Smith (12)
Trinity School, Carlisle

I HAD TO

Finally, I was about to win, but I didn't have the strength to kill Luke. Luke was lying there on the floor, I couldn't get myself to kill him. I helped Luke up and soon as he got up, he thanked me. I was thinking to myself it was a free hit, I could have killed him. The next day, I saw Luke running toward me. He had the look that he wanted to kill me. He swung at me but I blocked it, and then I took his head off. I did it to survive.

Freddie Newton (14)
Trinity School, Carlisle

HARLEY QUINN AND THE JOKER

The Joker met Harley Quinn. Harley was a normal lady that was a scientist. The Joker made Harley Quinn fall in love with him. Harley Quinn had pink and blue hair with an old T-shirt and a baseball bat she carried around. Harley Quinn had good in her, she just had to find it. Harley soon realised she had good in her, but let the Joker drag her down. He betrayed her. She became good. The Joker died and he couldn't bother her again.

Jasmine Marriott (12)
Trinity School, Carlisle

THE BOY WHO DIED

I still haven't forgotten the time when Harry defeated me. Snape had concocted a potion to give me a new resurrection stone. The more people I kill, the more powerful I get. Finally, I can get my revenge. I immediately know who to kill first, Harry Potter. I cast the Dark Mark in the sky so Harry can say his final goodbyes with a warning. After ten years, the time has come. It's time for my enemy to die...

Josie Bell (12)
Trinity School, Carlisle

BATHSEBA

I still haven't forgotten about that day. One morning, I woke up around 5:15, like every morning. I went on a walk to see my neighbour. I got told to go to the police office because I apparently put a needle in a child's head. I told them I didn't do it but they believed me. Everyone started to hate me for the rest of my life. Everyone will remember my name for the rest of their lives: Bathseba.

Lily Marskell (14)
Trinity School, Carlisle

EARTHQUAKES

Hello, my name is Earthquake. I'm about four billion years old. Those annoying humans build things on me and it hurts. So, I send earthquakes up to crush those structures. But there is a place I can't reach and they've beaten me to it. So, they started building big structures and as you may understand, it's endless pain for me. But, I've found a solution. If I stop sending earthquakes I can gather a big one and destroy everything they've built. So, in a couple of million years, I will destroy everything they've built. They're done for, mwahaha!

Alexander Carter (11)
Tuxford Academy, Tuxford

SPIDER

There I was, walking around a human's house, not knowing what was going to happen. Then I heard an intense scream behind me. "Argh! Spider!" A giant shoe was getting slammed onto the floor as they tried to kill me. The more I ran, the more tired I got. The more they attacked, the more I ran. The more they screamed, the more I questioned. *Was I the bad guy?* I thought while still running. *I didn't do anything wrong, did I?* Then, *boom*. Gone. Squished, dead. I died without knowing why, without knowing what I had done wrong.

Charlie Sharman (11)
Tuxford Academy, Tuxford

THE WOLF

"Wolf, come here." I turned to see who it was. It was Mum. "Come on, it's dinner time."
"Alright, Mum, coming," I replied.
A lovely smell arose from the plate in front of me. Rabbit, fresh from the meadow. Dad said he was going out. As he stepped outside, a gunshot rang out. Mum ran outside shouting Dad's name. A second shot followed, then all was silent. I ran outside to see an old woman with a rifle on her shoulder, walking away with my parents. I would get that woman, I would eat Grandma and I would get revenge.

Jack Martin (13)
Tuxford Academy, Tuxford

VICTIM

Five years and I'm still 'the bad guy'. No one knows the real truth but me. Not a single being. People know me as 'the big bad wolf', but no one knows I'm the actual *real* good guy. Here's my story and the true one at that. Us wolves lived in peace, living off the countryside, when one day everything changed. People! For whatever reason humans all of a sudden arrived. First, there were shouts and then gunshots, *Bang!* Eventually, all wolves were killed but me. I was in hiding when one day, a girl, Little Red, came...

Neve Littlewood (13)
Tuxford Academy, Tuxford

PRISON NOTES

Being fabulous and fashionable has its perks. Like creating a fake persona and ID without any police trace. And kidnapping my psychotic mother's dog fur coats. Despite all that, I still ended up in prison just like my mother. I was hoping to see her again, just so I could rub my success in her snooty face. Success came along with its own friend, jealousy. It seemed that everyone that was intimidated by me came along with jealousy. I remember meeting a girl in my fashion company called Anita, just like my old friend, Anita Darling, my beloved photographer.

Leah Wall
Tuxford Academy, Tuxford

THE ANDROID'S LAST FAILURE

I still haven't forgotten that traitorous assistant for attempting to destroy my code for good. I'm glad I had a backup in my lair, this is the final straw. It is time, I will activate the moderately underpowered death laser, aka MUDL. There is not stopping me. It has to update. Why, how? I am in space, how is it going to update? Fine, I'll wait. No, god, no! How did he find me, why? He ain't no Superman, he can't even breathe, guess I'll have to finish him. Glad I don't need to breathe to go and finish him.

Luke Shirley (13)
Tuxford Academy, Tuxford

I'M JUST MISUNDERSTOOD

Why did it happen? Why me, Alex Banderon, a sweet, happy, innocent, middle school boy that caught a deadly disease and died? Hi, I'm Death and my job is to, well, kill people. Just wait before you judge me, I never wanted to become Death, the guy everyone hates and misunderstands. I wanted to be a scientist that would cure cancer, but no, a disease had to come and kill me. If you're wondering how I got picked from the hat of 1000000 names, it's pretty simple, I died on the 1st of January 2011, at 00:01, aka, Death Day.

Abbie Flear (13)
Tuxford Academy, Tuxford

THE STORY BEHIND THE VILLAIN

Boom, one shot, *boom*, then another. The two bodies lying dead, the baby crying. From that moment on, he would never be the same. Grew up homeless, never loved again, never went to school, never had friends, always lonely. People do desperate things because of someone they love. Villains may not seem who they are. There is a story behind everything in this. He went on to rob banks and risk his life. He was never brought up, he was called the Joker. A mastermind involved in crime and a life no one would ever want.

Charles Doughty (12)
Tuxford Academy, Tuxford

IN THE WOODS

One day, I went to the woods to play hide-and-seek with my friends. I counted to ten whilst the others hid. I went to find them but they were nowhere to be seen. I started to panic. As time ticked by, my heart started to race. I looked around and saw trees and leaves aside from a small scary shadow. I walked closer and started to feel dizzy. As I got about two metres away, the shadow moved. I wondered what was going to happen next. As I approached, the shadow ran away. Oh no, what happened to hide-and-seek?

Erin Burke (12)
Tuxford Academy, Tuxford

MISUNDERSTOOD

I loved the world when I was younger, but the world didn't love me. I watched my best friend die in my arms, slipping away. That is so traumatic when it happens, the world feels more lonely than ever. But, you see, who cares? Nobody did for me. They didn't even consider what I felt, so I made them feel it. I took their best friends' lives. I am not a monster, I just wanted someone to be there for me, but they weren't. If they had only had my back, I wouldn't have become who I am now.

Anna Wheat (12)
Tuxford Academy, Tuxford

THE BRINGER OF DEATH

My plan was in motion. Fear was etched in every line of his face. Wind whipped my cloak about my face as I chased him. As I caught up, the screeches of fearful prey echoed around the clearing. With one slash, he crumbled to the floor. Gone. People would say I'm the bad guy, but I only end the suffering. The cries of angry voices could be heard in the distance, signifying it was my time to go. Being the bringer of death is a lot harder than being the giver of life, it's a job that must be done.

Evie Howarth (12)
Tuxford Academy, Tuxford

THE WITCH WHO KIDNAPPED CHILDREN

I was alone in the forest for years, no one knew I existed until one day, I saw these kids poking around my gingerbread house, but suddenly, I heard a big bang. My fence came crashing down. I ran outside and snatched the kids, I was going to get them to pay for what they did. Three months later, I fed them every week to make them fatter, and one day, I decided to open the fireplace and chuck them inside. Soon as I let go of them, the children's hands reached out and pulled me in too.

Isabela Hull (12)
Tuxford Academy, Tuxford

REVENGE

It's been years since my plans failed. After I lost that fight against my arch-enemy, Harvey. I was forced to flee to America and disguise myself as a Starbucks worker. Cold, dark and alone, I spend my days waiting for the day I can get my revenge. Then one day, I saw him again. Harvey.

"Andy, is that you?" he said.

"You rat," I snapped back.

"Excuse me?"

"Don't act dumb."

"Is this because I stole your sandwich at work?"

"You defeated me in a fight!"

"You tripped over your cape!"

"*Lies!*"

"Stop being dramatic, Andy."

Then he walked away...

Amy Peacock
West Kirby School & College, West Kirby

RIDDLER

People tell tales about the bad guys being bad but, this tale is not going to be that.

I started my evil venture on a barge, looking for a sword of darkness, on the deck of the black sparrow. I was so close to the sword unit...

The cave came in and we were lost forever in the darkness. A man came forth from the dark and told us, "I can only live where there is light, but die if light shines on me. What am I?"

The sword went to dust, so it was the voice in the dark.

Riley D (15)
West Kirby School & College, West Kirby

DR EVIL'S PART-TIME JOB

A Saturday night. Normal and calm. But in the local chippy, there was cause for alarm. A mysterious bald man serving fried fish. And his peculiar small friend washing a dish. "Hello, what's your order?" rings out from inside as Doctor Evil's plan has surely died. He never meant to be serving the local folk. He tried to destroy the world, but he ended up a joke.

But all is not lost down by the sea. As he still has his faithful companion, mini me.

Breandán Grady (14)
West Kirby School & College, West Kirby

ABLAZE

I lingered, my bearskin boots frozen in place, as the boat rocked softly side-to-side, the red-tinged ocean lapping peacefully below. Before me, on the bruised shore, lay a spectacle of utter destruction and despair; clusters of fire plagued the land as children cried out, desperately - hopelessly - for their parents. Mothers agonised over their homes, husbands and, ultimately, their hope - all lost to the catastrophe that was us Vikings. This couldn't be right. Even the farms, once luscious, reeked of ash, scarred by battle. Volleys of flaming arrows ruthlessly battered the Earth like an off-beat drum. For the first time, silence.

Jessica Kerry (15)
XP School, Doncaster

IVOK

This warrior is revengeful... After losing his authentic mighty older brother, he only thinks of vengeance. This inhibits his thoughts to become a bloodthirsty menace, only desiring the end of the Stoick Tribe, preventing love and compassion he once had. This is why he's here today, with his own tribe, on a homicidal field infused with screams of the death of reckless young and old, courageous warriors. Cold blood fills the air. Weapons, armour and gold scattered endlessly along the poignant scene of distress and anguish. Suddenly, Ivok makes eye contact with the man who brutally murdered his loving brother...

Aaron Twell (15)
XP School, Doncaster

REVENGE

I'm strolling through the primitive village I just single-handedly demolished. The overwhelming stench of burning flesh fills my nostrils; mothers still desperately crying out for their children. Out of the shadows appears a villager with a distressed face; they block my path, stumbling on their words, but shortly come to an abrupt stop, tumbling to the floor. I pick up my hand-crafted knife, wipe off the blood and carry on with my journey, my face inscrutable. I should feel remorse. I should feel pity. But I don't. I'm not done with my revenge yet. I've not even started. I smile...

Kiera Leaver (14)
XP School, Doncaster

AGAINST THE ODDS

Stepping onto the longboat, the overwhelming feeling of accomplishment rushed over me, realising that all the countless arguments and one-sided discussions with the chief finally paid off. The never-ending, stubborn responses of shaking heads, rolling eyes and no, no, nos finally led to a reluctant yes. I don't think I'll ever be able to forget that moment, the amount of pure joy rushing through me as soon as the words left his mouth; I felt I could have fainted then and there. Nearly did. But now I look around at the vast stretching sea, thinking of the endless possibilities ahead...

Nada Abdelbari (14)
XP School, Doncaster

THE RAID

"*To battle!*" I roared, my ship landing hurriedly on the shore with a crash. We finally arrived on the coast of England, ready to plunder all the shining silver we could find. We charged at the monastery, waving our axes savagely, preparing for a fight. The guards drew their blades in a feeble attempt to defend their land. After a bloody clash of steel and iron, the monastery was now unprotected. We forced the great oak door open and greedily seized the treasure inside. I, Jarl Halfdan Ragnarsson of Kattegat, proudly led my people to glory and riches that day.

Marcus Hague (15)
XP School, Doncaster

LOOKING OUT

Pressure. It might not be uttered amongst my folk, but it is surely amidst us. Standing here where my father, my grandfather, and many chiefs before him have all stood. Upon this hill: the highest point of the island. Rolling hills, lapping waves, farmers' fields filled with livestock. Stunning, breathtaking, remarkable. Standing here, trying to absorb the advice from all of my ancestors' souls present; alone but far from lonely. My only hope is that when it's my time to set sail on my final journey from this place, I will be remembered righteously.

Ebony Robins (15)
XP School, Doncaster

THE TRUTH BEHIND THE LIES

I suddenly heard the sound of distant carnage and people screaming in agony. I warned the village and prepared for confrontation. I walked through the village, the ground was shaking, I could smell smoke from burning corpses. They were right around the corner, I could hear the screams of death from all of the innocent people they had killed.
I stood strong and ready to defend my village. As they stopped, they saw we were stood, sentinel. Their faces dropped. They started to quiver in fear in our presence. We assembled our warriors and we were ready to fight!

Faith Farmery (14)
XP School, Doncaster

WHO AM I AND WHAT HAVE I BECOME?

I overlook the destruction around me, bloodthirsty monsters swarming everywhere. I'm portrayed just like them, a vicious, crazed beast, but that's not me. I don't want to take these innocent lives and I don't want to perish. My legs go paralysed as I look at the lifeless bodies surrounding me. I instantly feel nauseated and begin to regret my choices. Why am I here? This is not me. But I must become what I'm portrayed as to be honoured and dine the fine cuisine in Valhalla. I look at the sky while silently praying for the gods to take me.

Yasmin Ward (15)
XP School, Doncaster

202

THE ROOTS OF YGGRASIL

As I lie in my grave, I ponder whether I died a warrior's death. Indeed I did die in a battle, but it was my own inability to swim not in combat as the hull of our ship was destroyed. As I lie there, pondering upon this fact, a Valkyrie came and lifted me up out of my grave. I'm hopeful as I rise out of my grave, but then I'm plunged down so far I can see Jormungandr coiled around Midgard and I'm hopelessly dragged past all other realms. To Hell's frozen gate. Within the roots of Yggrasil...

Joshua Kitching (15)
XP School, Doncaster

LETTERS OF LOVE AND SORROW

This was the day. The day I was dreading. I stood by the sea, sand in-between my toes, fresh wind in my hair, as I watched the boats sail into the horizon. This may have been the last goodbye I ever said to my dearest Erik. We have only been married for two summers and Freya was still only an infant. Freya was stood staring into the distance alongside me. I didn't want for this to be the last time he saw her, but the village knew full well that it may be. For now, we watched from a distance...

Francesca Wileman (14)
XP School, Doncaster

DEATH AND DESTRUCTION

The wind is howling as I get ready for the fight of my life in the village of Norguard. Surrounded by beauty, only death awaits.

As my friends and I prepare for battle, I hear screams coming from outside of my longhouse. All around me are signs of death. My friends lie dying on the ground. I run towards my family, my wife and child! Fear pouring from the sweat escaping my body.

Please let them be safe...

Joshua Waszak (14)
XP School, Doncaster

YoungWriters Est. 1991

YOUNG WRITERS INFORMATION

We hope you have enjoyed reading this book – and that you will continue to in the coming years.

If you're a young writer who enjoys reading and creative writing, or the parent of an enthusiastic poet or story writer, do visit our website **www.youngwriters.co.uk**. Here you will find free competitions, workshops and games, as well as recommended reads, a poetry glossary and our blog. There's lots to keep budding writers motivated to write!

If you would like to order further copies of this book, or any of our other titles, then please give us a call or order via your online account.

Young Writers
Remus House
Coltsfoot Drive
Peterborough
PE2 9BF
(01733) 890066
info@youngwriters.co.uk

Join in the conversation!
Tips, news, giveaways and much more!

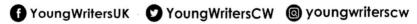

YoungWritersUK · YoungWritersCW · youngwriterscw